A CHORUS OF WOLVES

STORIES

ALEX KIMMELL

booktrope

Booktrope Editions
Seattle WA 2013

Cover Design by Greg Simanson

Edited by Katrina M. Randall

This is a work of fiction. Names, characters, places, brands, media, and incidents are either the product of the author's imagination or are used fictitiously. Any resemblance to similarly named places or to persons living or deceased is unintentional.

PRINT ISBN 978-1-62015-183-9
EPUB ISBN 978-1-62015-279-9

For further information regarding permissions, please contact info@booktrope.com.

Also by Alex Kimmell:

the Key to everything

Thank You Dad

For teaching me there is art in everything

…and how to know it when I find it

I miss you

CONTENTS

THE GIRL WHO FELL THROUGH

Ladies of a Death Man
One

"Good love is hard to find."

—*TOM PETTY*

MY NAME IS PALL. I'm Death. No, really. I met your great grandparents and their great grandparents too. I even know some of your parents and your friends. Sucks for you, but it's kind of my job. That made me sound like an asshole. Sorry. I'm really a pretty nice guy. That is, when I'm a guy. I've been female on occasion. I try to appear in such a way that my customers will be comfortable as possible. See? I'm nice. Right?

My job's pretty cool. I've seen the entire world and I get to know lots of people. Every person at some point actually. The hours are tough. I don't get too many breaks and I can't remember my last long vacation. But, I think I spent it someplace cold and unpopulated. I like snow. It's pretty.

Building a social life is tough in this job. I can't stay in one place for too long, so forming a lasting relationship becomes quite the challenge. Though, the past few years did make things a little easier for me. The Internet with email and social networking sites help out a lot. I can drop into my network on my phone whenever I want, no matter where I am. Plus I can check my schedule to see who lives near where I'm going to be, whenever I do get some down time.

I don't date much unfortunately. I'd like to. Most people get freaked out when they read the job description on my profiles. I have one set up as a man and the other one is, well, you know. In case you're wondering, I filled them out truthfully. Mistake number one. The parade of synapse misfires that contacted me seemed never ending.

There was this Goth chick named Psycofantia with the obvious rebellion tattoos, studs in her cheeks and the ever so attractive anarchy symbol implant under the skin of her forehead. She liked to play Russian roulette with a Colt 45 shoved up her cooter. "Am I gonna die now?" Click. "How about now?" click. When the gun misfired, she actually got pissed off at me that she didn't die.

You must have seen reports in the news about that priest who raped the little blind children in Texarkana? Remember the lawyer who worked diligently to make sure his client wasn't convicted? Yeah, that scumbag asked me to meet him in a no-tell on Pleasantville Pike North-west of Providence. He took off every scrap of clothing but a three hundred dollar pair of custom made shoes. He was reflective as a calm lake at dawn before the first breath of wind ripples over the surface. The freshly shaved skin of his shins scabbed from razor cuts was still moist. I know this because he didn't wear socks. He wanted me to iron his black, custom tailored suit, fold the creases neatly and rest it gently on top of the motel dresser. He hung himself from a scratchy, frayed rope tied to a hook that we screwed into the ceiling. When I left he was still dangling there, fingers furiously tugging at his unimpressively small mutton dagger.

Abnormally Dissolved Foetus, a really shitty Scandinavian death metal band responded to my Craigslist ad inviting me to a show in the Oliwa forest outside of Gdansk. They were set up in an area littered with crosses and stone covered grave mounds on a dark, storm encrusted night. Of course they were. Where else would they be?

Bare trees wrapped prison bar branches around shirtless, tribal tattooed band members in the glacial winter air. Puffing steam clouds, the five Neanderthals ramrodded their detuned dirge in a tripping rhythm. Long-haired heads slammed to the war march of stone drunk zombified pedophile rhinoceros trainers. No discernible division barred the band and their congregation of naked converts, bodies painted in thick, crumbling, repellant white from head to toe. Some bled from fresh, self-inflicted wounds on their arms and stomachs.

A muddy, dreadlocked girl, not more than fifteen or sixteen decided it would be a good idea to grind her way to happy town on the jagged remains of a decomposing tree stump. Keep in mind, being who I am, and doing what I do I've witnessed a lot of foul looking shit. The results of her Cardinal paying a visit during that Jill off session with the tree, made me reassess a few things about how the homo sapien has degenerated.

Flailing their crusty-white limbs in orgiastic circles around a blazing fire built near the original spot of the devil's stone before it rolled into the river, they showed no fear of me. They growled along, throwing the youngest into the licking tendrils of the enormous funeral pyre as sacrifices. Some made their way across by my side. Others remained breathing lumps of scar tissue that would last days, weeks or years until my next visit to their bedsides. Did I get laid? Was I offered a kiss or an embrace? Not even a high five. In other words, they weren't interested in my need to be loved. They contacted the job, not the person. My hide chapped.

More and more the responses to my ads descended into loathsome samples of human refuse. Prisoners with life sentences for crimes committed against former clients of mine looking for a digital pen pal to exchange dirty notes and pictures with. A hopelessly inept hit man tried bribing me to finish off an annoyingly difficult and dangerously deranged school teacher-raping son of a New Jersey drug kingpin to free himself up for a trip to Burning Man with his boyfriend. A shunned and distraught chess club member and first time broken hearted teenager searching for a way out of her oppressively abusive home life, shot me a brief email (with explicitly detailed photos attached) after slitting her stepfather's wrists while he was on a nightly bender in the bathtub. I became a shrink. Not really my thing you know? Even if my only goal was some vaginal bungee jumping, it could not have been more damn frustrating. Like Freddie sang, "Can anybody find me somebody to love?"

So, learning from past mistakes, I went back online and built new profiles. I wanted to weed out at least a top layer of previously mentioned freaks and morbid fanatics. Of course I was still interested in a bit of bone smuggling, so the temptation to enhance my personality into a gorgeously larger than life, millionaire jet-setting international fuck toy pulled hard at my fingers on the touchscreen. Adjusting to modern day Internet etiquette parameters, I allowed myself to bend the truth in small amounts rather than breaking it into shattered pieces that barely resembled me. Besides, I longed for a deeper and more meaningful relationship than some shame inducing day tripper.

At first glance, her response didn't jump out at me from the screen. My pulse remained slow and steady, failing to quicken at the mere thought of meeting some divine creature who, through some miracle of the cyberspace love machine, could be "the one." The email said exactly this:

> Hi. I like your ad. You seem like the right balance of a-hole and boringness. I'm snarky and kind of a bitch. Shoot me a note and let's see if I don't hate you.

No misspelled words, hyphenated profanity and openly admitted that she was a bitch. Three check marks in the plus column. But if the contents of the message itself didn't inspire me to respond, her email address did: seeyounexttuesdaymd@bitchyness.org I hearted her the moment it flashed in my lonely inbox.

Our correspondence started boringly enough with some simple exchanges of "hellos" and "getting-to-know-each-others" every few days. She sent a note about how much she hated her job at Saint John's Hospital Emergency Room. There were too many patients dying from easily cured diseases and injuries lately. Of course I knew this all too well having visited there on a relatively frequent basis. I didn't try to spy on her, honestly. When I'm called, I go, whenever and wherever it is. That's the gig. I'd wait a day or two, send a reply with no details offered to describe my own employment situation, which she showed no interest in anyway.

I'd had a shit day the first time we talked on the phone. Even for me. I'm used to the punching, kicking, scratching, biting and screaming when I show up. You see, people fall into a handful of distinct categories when I visit them.

1. **The Criers** - Self-explanatory.

2. **The Screamers** - My ears have bled from the intense volume levels of some of the whining.

3. **The Angry** - I've been kicked in my Ken/Barbie doll private blank spaces on more than one occasion.

4. **The Beggars** - These ramblers think that getting on their knees can actually change what has to happen to them.

5. **The Deniers** - Unfortunately for these guys, I don't make mistakes at work. (Only in private.)

6. **The Believers** - Religious/faithful types who honestly think they are off to meet God.

7. **The Lawyers** - Let's make a deal! Um…no.

8. **The Unconscious** – Those without enough developed individualized consciousness to notice the difference between being alive and being…you know. Infants mostly. Or those too old and lost to understand what's happening.

9. **The Lickity Splitters** – Happy to see me coming, "What took you so long?" and "I'm ready to get the fuck out of dodge!" type folks.

10. **The Accepters** – Fully aware and understanding that I am inevitable. I am as much a part of life as breathing. Nothing can prevent or postpone my arrival, so I am welcomed with open arms and a loving, calm embrace.

Every century or so, I am caught off guard. Sometimes it's on a battlefield. It can be a king in his golden bed or a homeless drifter riding a box car across Tuscaloosa. On this particular day the eight year old boy lay in the blue racecar bed in the cancer ward at Johns Hopkins, holding his sleeping mother's hand after an endlessly long day of chemotherapy.

"Shh." He looked me straight in the eye. "Don't wake up Mommy. She's tired."

"I'll be quieter than air." I thought about a wink and a smile, but this child looked at me as I am. He didn't need to see a clown or cartoon character to feel reassured. I hid behind no mask of skin and bone.

"It's okay. Don't be sad." In the most unfair of unfair moments, he reached for me with his free hand to do the unimaginable. The boy comforted me. My non-existent lungs shuddered in an agonizingly woeful breath. I sniffled through a nose that wasn't there. "Don't be sad." Right then, at that moment I hated my job. More than ever before, since the beginning of beginning, I hated my fucking job. "Please make sure Mommy's happy without me."

This is a small glimpse into why my mood sucked pretty hard that night. This kid who never stood a chance at any kind of life other than his short time spent doing nothing but suffering in pain, had more empathy and kindness than I'd seen possible in centuries of memory. It was my job to cleave him away from his loving mother into the dusty randomness of infinity for no reason that I could explain. So, I was upset to say the least.

"Hey there." I couldn't put a face to the voice on my phone. I'd heard her speak in the hospital, but never on the line before.

"Yeah?" I spit the bullet words out. "Who is it?"

"Wow. Grumpy much?" The rapidly returned fire didn't hesitate turning me back on the defensive. "It's Liné. You gave me your number yesterday. Unless you didn't expect me to use it?"

"Oh. Hi." Unsure of how to regain my composure and display some semblance of cool, I tried lowering my voice. "Today took a crapper on my head and left no paper to wipe."

"Hmm." She didn't sound impressed. "Strike one."

"Strike one?"

"It's a metaphor." I heard her spit and roll a window up. "You know, like in baseball? Three strikes and yer out?"

"Didn't realize I made it up to the plate."

"Hey," I could feel her finger inching closer to the End Call button on her phone. "If you want to go back in the dugout, it's easily arranged."

"Very funny."

"No joke." A car door shut and hard-soled shoes echoed over a hard surface. "I don't have time for assholes."

"I know." I became an elementary school pipsqueak trying not to hand my lunch money over to the schoolyard troll. "I know."

"Do you?"

"Yes."

"Do you really?"

"So I'm not allowed to have a bad day?" I felt testicles descend out of the previously genderless area between my legs.

"Nope."

"Wow. Have a nice life then." I wanted to hang up. I really did. I would have too, but she laughed and my thumb hesitated.

"I'm twisting your nips Pally." I didn't remember telling her my name. It had to be on my profile though. "Sorry you had a bad day. Anything I can do?"

"No." Her keys jingled and another door opened in the background followed by a soft ding.

"Well, I'm about to get on the elevator. Dinner? Tomorrow night?" Sounded good to me. Food in a public place? No autoerotic asphyxiation or group-sacrifice rituals.

"How's Fritto Misto on 4th Street?" I picked a place I knew was small and quiet. Good food too. "Say around nine?"

"See you then." Her shoes clicked on a softer floor. "Have a better day tomorrow Pall." I listened to the dial tone hearing the billions of voices traveling through the atmosphere behind the buzz. Then I needed to be in South Africa for another pickup. The old woman's curious look pulled me back into the moment, wiping the smile from my face as I swung the scythe into the side of her neck.

"So what's it like to be dead?"

"Don't know."

"What do you mean you don't know?"

"I'm not dead. I'm Death. There's a bit of a difference."

"Like?"

"I still exist. I haven't died. I'm Charrion. I bring anyone alive to the other side."

"Interesting. Lame. But interesting."

"Lame?"

"Yeah it is."

"Fuck you."

"I mean seriously? You're Death and you don't even know what being dead means?"

"Sure I do."

"Okay. Tell me then."

"It's not something that can be put into words."

"You are so full of shit."

"I'm being serious."

"So am I."

"Can we drop it please?"

"No. Was Dante right? Was Milton? Christians, Jews, Muslims? What happens on the 'other side'?"

"I don't know."

"Right."

"Not my job."

"So what? It's not my job to drive a cab, but I know what they do."

"Not the same thing and you know it."

"Haven't you ever asked your boss?"

"Don't have one."

"You don't have a boss?"

"Nope."

"What about God?"

"What *about* God?"

"Who tells you who to pick up next? Where to go? What to do?"

"Nobody."

"So how do you know?"

"I just do."

"That doesn't make any sense."

"Does it need to?"

"I…"

"Look, we're talking about insubstantialities here. Things that have no business being described. Things that aren't supposed to be explained as easily as what goes into making your breakfast sausage. Fact is, I'm here. I do what I do. I've always done it. I always will. Life is a finite experience. It has a beginning and an end. Why? Don't know, don't care. Philosophers can question it as much as they want. Won't change the facts that there's black and white, day and night, life and death."

"Life and you."

"Yeah. Life and me. Here we are. Are you gonna eat that cheesecake? It's wheat free."

"Are there any others like you?"

"What do you mean?"

"Any other 'Deaths'? You can't be responsible for every single death in history. Can you?"

"Hmm. Never thought about it."

"Unless time moves at a different pace for you than it does for the rest of us."

"I don't think it does."

"So there must be other Deaths out there somewhere."

"I guess."

"You guess?"

"I never met any of them if that's what you mean."

"Don't you think people have 'crossed over' that you weren't responsible for? Like soldiers on a battlefield or victims of a cholera epidemic?"

"Now that you mention it…"

"This can't be the first time you're thinking about this."

"Gee, forgive a guy for being fucking busy. I spend all my time flicking around the world. Here, there and everywhere without a second to myself. I don't get much time to sit on my ass pondering the secrets of existence like you do."

"Sorry. I didn't mean to offend you."

"No. Just belittle everything I do. Anyone can do it. There's thousands of others all over the place doing the same thing as me. Just like that. Simple as apple fucking pie."

"That's not what I meant."

"Right. I think this date's over. I'll see you again when it's your time. If not me, it'll be one of the other Deaths doing the job I can't do by myself because I'm too fucking lazy."

"Wait…"

I left. Not through the door of course. I can make an awesome exit when I want to. No cloud of smoke or pop of displaced air crashing together. When I want to be gone, I'm gone. The bitch wouldn't be forgetting me any time soon.

I buried myself in work for the next day or two. Pardon the pun. The usual jobs in hospitals, retirement homes and South Los Angeles gang territory. When I went to a hurricane devastated city in southern Indonesia, Liné's observation of my limitations squeezed into focus. Thousands of people were ready. I could see them waiting for me to come. All radiated the soft, black glow of expiration used for eons as a beckoning symbol. For the first time I noticed that only a handful of them looked directly at me. For the first time I watched the eyes of other soon-to-be passengers staring in other directions.

I took the hands of my guests one at a time and sent them on their way. Some one's, four's and five's, a dozen two's and a few hundred three's. When I finished, I didn't leave to go to my next appointment. I waited and watched. More of the dead were gone than I had escorted. Bodies littered the buildings and village streets that had no connection to me. Liné was right after all. There had to be more Deaths than just me. I expected to feel dejected. I waited for depression to smother me in a cold blanket of shame and uselessness.

It didn't come. Instead, showers of exhilaration bucketed down from the storm clouds hovering over the city. I laughed. Echoes of my joy bounded off broken walls and through cracked windows. I hunched over while the muscles of my mid-section tightened and unclenched uncontrollably. Weights of relief fell in piles from my burdened shoulders crashing through the ground into a vast wasteland of useless negativity.

Catching my breath, I dialed the phone. I needed to apologize.

"Liné, it's me. Pall. You were right. There are more." I rambled on her voicemail for minutes, talking and talking. Words disgorged from my lips with no breaths in between. A tributary of scarcely distinguishable words smudged together. I think it was all in English. I won't bore you with the whole thing. Just the end: "I'm a dick. Please call me back. I need to see you."

The knowledge that others were out there doing the same work as me stripped away a layer of guilt in taking some personal time. If there were more Deaths, they could take up some of the slack I might leave behind when I took a day off. Maybe even a weekend. Hell, I could take a week. A week! Imagine that, seven whole days with nothing to do. The possibilities left my egg brain scrambled.

"I don't trust the metric system." Her face was cold and unreadable.

"Why not?" Coffee spilled between my lips, falling over my chin to stain the front of my clean white shirt. The used paper towels piled up around my half-eaten breakfast plate and made a small mound of tannish white clinging to the legs of my chair. "I'm sure it's been plotting the fall of democracy along with that rat bastard Jimmy Carter and the entire Spanish language."

"I'm completely serious." Leaving the last fork full of eggs on her plate, she pushed it away from the edge of the table.

"That's just stupid."

"So you think I'm stupid?"

"Not at all. I think a mistrust of measurements isn't the most rational choice, but you're definitely not stupid." I let go from restraining myself. I knew the can was open now and there was no way I could close it without getting into a fight.

"You can't have it both ways." She leaned back in her chair, arms folding across her chest. Bars were up, windows locked, jaw clenching loaded for bear.

"Sure I can." The towel spun off the roll. Unless she had a stain remover in her laundry room, this Rorschach mark on my stomach wasn't going away.

"That's not fair."

"I can have an opinion about an isolated statement you make that doesn't relate to my opinion about you." Logic. Would it work?

"If that statement is part of my belief system, you can't separate it from who I am as a person." Nope. The thinking approach wasn't happening.

"Don't be so black and white about it Liné." My chair scraped over the linoleum floor. "We aren't covered in map lines. The world isn't fair."

"Fuck you it's not." Her head shook. I watched the back of her neck turn red standing in front of the sink throwing dishes.

"It isn't." The shovel refused to stop digging.

"Don't be such a whiney little pussy." Turning around in attack mode, the sneer stretched nearly every trace of grace from her cheeks. "I mean, look at what you do. You take children from their mothers, husbands from wives. You don't discriminate between evils and innocents."

"Screw you." That blow landed square in my gut, drawing every last bit of wind from my lungs.

"Fine. Screw me. But the world is completely fair. Anyone who says it isn't needs to grow a pair, rub some dirt on it and get back in the game." Who knew she liked sports?

"The world isn't the Super Bowl. You can't by tickets." I wanted to wave the white flag. Instead the drill bit dove deeper into the shit.

"I know. You have to *steal* them." I'd have felt safer with the Craigslist freaks at this point.

"Wow. You really are a bitch you know?" Deeper and deeper.

"Proud to be." I could see the muscles tense in her arms. She needed to let it all out now. Blow it up and burn everything down.

I laughed at my own role in the irony. "I don't get it. How can you say the world is fair? There's so many people starving and..."

"...Homeless and killed by tyrants and are lonely with no one to love. Boo fucking hoo. Stop complaining about how hard things are. Stop feeling sorry for yourself and everybody else that doesn't get exactly what they want the instant they want it.

"Difficult? Yeah. Challenging? Obviously. Life is the hardest thing there is. This place? This... planetgalaxyuniverse? It's created to fight you. With one sole purpose..." She took a long sip from her coffee and glared out the window. "...to knock everything away from your greedy little fingers, to rip the food right out of your mouth.

"We all started from an explosion. Hell, we're still exploding. Explosions don't give a rat's about fairness or equality. Yeah, it's all fucked up." She continued ranting at the universe. I might as well have not even been in the room. "Nobody in the government wants to save your poor little life. Folks on the street don't waste a second thought on you when they kick the crutches out from under your arms. People aren't good. People are *ambivalent*. Unless it comes to where our next meal is coming from or if somebody else fucks someone we want to fuck, we don't really give a shit. We are all bought and sold man. We need to buy the newest, latest and greatest shiny piece of crap so we can impress everyone else who still has last year's shiny piece of crap. We need to be skinny, have longer hair, listen to the right music, watch the most popular shows....

"None of it makes any real difference. It's all an act. It's the wool covering our eyes. It's the security blanket that keeps us safe from how fucking hard everything is. That doesn't mean it's not fair. Fair is for three year olds and fairy tales. Fair ain't real Pall."

She motioned for me to slide my chair away from the table and sat in my lap. After showing the ability she had to be so aggressive, the gentleness of her fingers through my hair washed my defenses away and made me love her that much more. I didn't know kisses could be that deep.

"You can yell as loud as you want. I still think you're wrong."

"Shut up and take me to the bedroom."

Liné looked past the robe and scythe image. She took time to understand me. We walked along the beach under clouded stars digging our toes into the Santa Monica sands. I nursed my Pale Ale while she ate an onion bagel and told me stories of growing up in Long Beach and medical school at UCLA. Nobody ever looked at me the way she did before. When our eyes met, she didn't turn away nervously or blink. She locked on and held tight.

I like to think of myself as a gentleman, at least when I'm a man. I don't like to kiss and tell, but she swept me away in a riptide stronger than any pull of moon to sea. Her hand reached the back of my neck pulling me close. Her lips force fed the emptiness inside with fervent, delectable morsels that I can still taste today. If I close my eyes I can feel her pressing into me, filling the need I hadn't grown fully aware of until that moment.

Duty called me away shortly after our first kissing session. The vastness of her understanding made it extremely difficult for me to leave. I'm certain that the next few weeks, customers could fill a gross number of complaint boxes if we provided them with the cards to assess my performance. Fortunately for me, it makes no real difference if I'm attentive to your needs or negligent and forceful. Her lips remained forefront in my mind. No cholera epidemic, war zone or cancer ward broke through my love struck haze.

Then she broke my heart. Yes, I do indeed have a heart. A pretty sensitive one though most people probably don't think so. In hindsight, I could have called or sent a message to her before I showed up in her apartment. Surprising her seemed like a lot more fun.

FYI, women don't like it when you talk about jerking off. Most of them anyway. They don't want to hear that you thought about their bouncy tits and round handful of ass when you last did it. Take care not to mention pictures of swimsuit edition supermodels or slutty co-ed ex-girlfriends you have stacked on deck in the masturbation rolodex of your mind either. That'll piss them off even more. Apparently women are sensitive about shit like that.

She had no qualms in making me jealous by talking about the actors, singers or athletes appearing behind her passionately closed eyelids during violently loud orgasms though. What would my feelings matter? After all, I'm only Death. Someone like me doesn't have feelings in the first place. Right?

I knew the layout of her place before we'd met. I shouldn't have read her mind when we kissed. I did it without thinking. Couldn't be helped. I faded into her bathroom hoping she wouldn't be using it at the time. I took off my cowl and hung it on the shower curtain rod. I checked myself in the mirror fixing the few stray hairs blown out of place from traveling so far. The dematerialization and rematerializing process can be much more blustery than most people think. Anyway, the comb hardly stuck through the first strands of hair when I heard the music. Sexy time music. A deep voice with wah wah guitars and slow tempo bass groove? Groovy porn type stuff.

She made primal, beastly noises. Far more whorish than the imagined sounds she'd make when we did it in my head. Instead of a quiet giggle, a screech, "Give me that big cock, fucker!" No halting breath inhaled at the height of ecstasy. She roared, "Spread me wide. Fill me up. Tear me apart. Fuck! Shit yeah! I'm gonna shove my tongue up your tight little ass pussyboy."

I was nonplussed. Unfortunately turned on, but pissed off. My first instinct was to break in on them. Confront her and kill him. Cross him over the dark threshold with the most pain and terror my powers allowed. Unfortunately, "Pussyboy" wasn't on my list for another twelve years, three months, one week, four days, seventeen hours and twenty two seconds. The car crash would kill him instantly, painlessly. Sometimes the universe really isn't fair.

He was not mine to take yet. Of course, he didn't know that. Looking through his mind, one lucky perk of my job, I searched for signs of dread. The nightmare visage he expected Death to assume when I came for him. Not the hooded skull waving his long, bloodied scythe. No snake-tongued, red-horned, pitch-forked, spike-tailed, fire-eyed demon with soulless eyes, either. Inspired by an unusually abusive pre-algebra teacher in middle school, the image of Pussyboy's greatest fear was a snaggle-toothed, bow-tied, ink-smeared coke bottle glassed tax accountant named Eugene.

What a Kodak moment! Wearing a red and yellow checkered bowtie, I stepped from the shadowed bathroom and revealed myself next to the shaking bed frame. His girlish screech rattled the sliding glass window.

"Boo." My whisper caught him more unprepared and he fell off the bed into the pile of impatiently disregarded clothes.

"How did you get in here Pall?" My image as the nerdy bookkeeper only appeared to the terrified "pussyboy," who at that moment scooped up his khakis in mid-flight to the exit. Liné saw the me she was used to seeing. "What the fuck man?"

"Thought I'd pop in for a surprise." I sat on the edge of the bed with my hands on my knees. "Guess the surprise was on me, huh?"

"You should've called first." The front door of her apartment slammed shut and she pulled the sheets over her chest.

"You think so?" Seething through my clenched teeth, my anger filled the room with a cloud of bitterness.

"What are you so mad about? It's not like we're exclusive or anything. Shit."

"Do you ever not swear?" My attention focused solely on one word rather than accept the rejection of her sentiment.

"Fuck you. Does that answer your question?" I could smell sulfur before the match struck. She dropped the remaining pack of cigarettes on the bed and inhaled deep. "I never explained myself to my Daddy. I'm not about to start now. So don't assume I feel guilty."

"Not the best tactic for a relationship with me Liné." I squeezed my hands ready to punch a hole through the nearest wall. "Making me angry is a bad idea."

"Don't threaten me Pall." Her chin jutted forward defiantly. "I'm not yours."

"Never thought you were." And I didn't. Problem was I was hers.

"You were out there somewhere killing people…"

"I never killed anybody."

"Whatever." At this point, it didn't matter what I did or didn't do. "I can fuck anybody I want."

"Sure you can."

"I can enjoy it too." Her voice grinned viciously.

"Stop."

"Don, that's the guy I was with tonight." She stood and walked to the closet.

"Stop."

"He wasn't the first guy since you left either." Her voice was muffled between the dresses and coats hanging next to each other.

"Please."

"He knew how to do it right though." The insectile chatter speak of hangers clicking together crawled over the floor and out of the deep closet. "I just might have him again later this week."

"Why are you doing this to me?"

Liné wrapped her arms around my waist from behind. She lifted her head next to my ear and whispered, "Why not?"

I wish I could say I didn't think about her much after that night. Of course I did. The moments you get your heart broken are recorded and filed away among the important events in your life like birth and of course, death. Two and a half years later I arrived at a secluded construction site near East Providence. Two large men stood with their backs to me. By the looks of it, the one on the right was holding a gun. A middle-aged man with a bad toupee faced them next to a woman crying in the other direction.

"Apparently Ms. Moniz doesn't like your stepping around." The hulk on the left grumbled.

"Guys, this can all be fixed up." The balding man with the bad lid chattered words through his lips like a woodpecker bouncing its head off a tree. "You work for me. Right?"

"Not tonight we don't." The gunslinger took a step forward and pressed the snub nosed barrel of his .38 into the center of the panicked man's forehead. "So shut up."

"Don't worry Mr. Moniz. We're not here to kill you." The other thug smiled. "Not tonight anyway." With that he placed his hand in between the woman's shoulder blades and shoved. Without a muffled squeak over the sweat sock stuffed in her mouth, she fell forward into a hole in the ground. "Get up in the mixer Mr. Moniz."

"What?" He looked at the two toughs in shock.

"Don't make me tell you again." The man waved his .38 in the direction of the cement mixer's driver side door.

"I can't." He shook his head.

"Yes you can." The two men picked him up and threw him behind the wheel. "You will or the girl gets some company down there."

"I don't know how." Mr. Moniz slobbered.

"You expect us to believe that you've been in the construction biz for twenty-five years and you don't know how to turn on a cement mixer?" The two guys looked at each other and laughed. "Bullshit. Press the button or I pull the trigger."

I dropped into the hole next to Liné. As soon as she saw me she stopped trying to climb her way out of the hole. Her cheek was puffy and red from a hard slap, but her eyes looked into mine with the same intensity I remembered. Still myself, she didn't need me to appear as anything but me. She smiled around the sock, ever the flirt. I shrugged my shoulders and left her there as the wet cement started to fall around her feet. Her screams disappeared shortly after the hole filled to the top.

Now and again I'll pass by that building. I can still hear her. Since I didn't take her, she'll always be there.

KODI

WE HAD TO SHIELD OUR EYES, the moon was so bright. So perfectly full and round, it reflected the light of the sun with such intensity that every blade of grass in the yard reached up to the sky in prayer. Leaves came back to the trees after a long, cold winter spent in hibernation and frogs were once again making their presence known in the neighborhood. We weren't exactly lulled to sleep by their guttural lullabies, but their repetitive croaking added to the white noise alongside the crickets and branches rustling in the mild spring breeze.

When we bought this land for our house, the stories came with it. The company that developed most other properties in the area avoided building on this particular spot. When surveying the land, the instruments never gave the same reading twice. Sometimes the distance between two trees appeared longer or the boulder sat higher on the rise than it did the previous afternoon.

You could see how it became problematic. The company's architects threw their hands up in frustration. Unable to obtain exact measurements made it impossible to design a fence let alone a house.

So many people passed on the place before Michelle and I came around that the price dropped low enough to make an asymmetrical structure seem worth it. Strangely enough, our architects never had a problem with their measurements.

Kodi slept on the porch having finished protecting us for the night from the dangers he smelled lurking behind every shadow. He was so big that most people thought he could be a bear rather than a dog. At three years old he weighed two hundred and fifty pounds, give or take. He was all muscle, solid black with a head as big as my chest. He was a sweetheart, though. Newfoundlands are known to be extremely family oriented and Kodi was no exception. He looked after us and loved us like we were his pack.

A few months ago, Michelle brought home one of her co-workers and her husband for dinner. It was pretty obvious from the get-go that this Prius driving, pocket protector geek was not a dog person at all. He saw the big black dog sitting protectively in front of the house and refused to get out of his car. I waved hello and walked Kodi into the backyard so our new guests would feel comfortable enough to come into the house.

Kodi lay down on the patio and watched us longingly through the bay window. He usually slept on my feet while we ate, so he was obviously confused as to why this night was different from all others. After dinner we went to the living room and loosened ourselves up with cocktails before dessert. Mr. Boring was telling us a story about how he broke his arm last summer falling off a ladder while cleaning the leaves out of his rain gutter. Ignoring the bright orange warning stickers, he apparently felt the need to stand on one of the highest steps in order to reach the drain with his small gardening trowel. As he acted out losing his balance, he whirled his arms in circles. Whipping around this way and that, he made a bad pseudo comical impression of a Danny Kaye dance routine.

Kodi obviously didn't know he was telling us a harmless story and perceived the frantic wind-milling arms as threatening gestures. Being protective as he was, he jumped and broke through the screen door sending shards of aluminum mesh and splinters of wooden framework flying. Growling with rage, he lunged at the hapless dog hater unlucky enough to be in the center of our living room. All black fur with drool flying everywhere, Kodi bared his teeth fiercely and pinned the poor skinny man to the wall. When Kodi stands on his hind legs he is nearly five and a half feet tall. He held the terrified man with paws on his shoulders and clenched fangs growling only inches from his face. I could simply give the word and no money in the world would have been able to put Humpty Dumpty's face back together again.

Instead, I yelled for the big dog to get down, once. Only once. Instantly, he dropped and sauntered over to me tail wagging. He rubbed up against my waist and looked up at me as if to say, "I saved you, Dad!" I would have laughed, but the sight of a darkening patch slowly spreading on the front of the shaken man's otherwise pristinely cleaned and pressed tan chinos halted me instantly. I pulled Kodi back out to the center of our yard chastising him as we went, and locked his tether onto the ring of his white collar.

By the time I got back into the house I could hear tires screeching on the driveway and the soft click of the lock sliding shut as the front door closed gently. Michelle stood with her back to the door, head up and eyelids down. She took in a deep breath through her nose, held it for a long time and exhaled slowly from between clenched teeth. I didn't say anything. I just shrugged my shoulders as she opened her eyes directly on me and shook her head.

A little while later, I dried my wrinkled hands after finishing the evening's dishes. While I hung the towel on the oven's bar handle, I looked out into the backyard where Michelle sat cross-legged in her white nightgown with the big, bad boy's head resting in her lap. She rubbed his ears absentmindedly and through the partially opened windows I could hear her singing to him. She had a rich, gravelly voice that always reminded me of old dirt country roads. Her version of "Whipping Post" was sad and mournful unlike the rage filled take the Allman Brothers gave it. I think that the giant black dog might have even been crying.

She finished the song; I opened the remains of the broken screen door and waited for her to kiss Kodi on the head and come back inside. "He feels bad enough Mark. He was only trying to protect us." I nodded and let my arm fall across her back as she wrapped herself into my body and pulled tight. "That's his job, right?"

I looked down into her gigantic green eyes and smiled. "Yeah, he's a good boy." We moved together back into the house and closed the splintered frame of the door behind us. "Still, he should sleep outside tonight just the same."

Michelle breathed a sigh and whispered, "Okay."

"I may have to take a drive with you to the office on Monday. Just so I can see what happens." There was silence for a moment. Then the room filled with echoes of our lung busting, heart-crackling laughter ricocheting between the walls.

We used to go for long, leisurely walks around the neighborhood. Since he always stayed at my side, I never put Kodi on a leash. He'd bump my leg to let me know when he needed a pee or a sniff of an interesting scent. The random rabbit or squirrel running across the street might tease a deep growl or earth-quaking bark, but he'd never pull to chase.

The day after a rain brought new smells from the soft dirt and fresh mud to roll around in. Kodi loved those days in particular. We turned north on Saint Mark's Road from Pastor Pike under the perfect cerulean sky with only slight hints of high clouds drifting lazily as reminders of the recent storm. He sniffed damp grass while I hummed the melody from a Paul Weller song my garage band played in high school.

None of the houses had fences around their yards save one. Most people in our neighborhood enjoyed the freedom of not being trapped on their property. Unfortunately, this particular family had a dog with a mean streak. Getting too close to their house meant teeth chomping and claws digging. More than a few kids on skateboards or bikes earned stitches and scars at 12 Saint Mark's. Calls to animal control and threats of lawsuits resulted in the ugly, too-tall wooden fence.

Passing casually on the opposite side of the street, the barking commenced before we passed the neighbor's house. Claws scratching at wooden posts were accompanied by fierce growls. Hints of dirt brown fur and yellowed teeth pushed through the spaces between. Salivating, angry and seething for a fight, pointed ears punctuated the air above the fence top dying to make it over to the other side.

A gunshot crack pierced the air. Pounding at the splintered shards of wood, the German Shepard forced his way through to the open grass slicing its ribs along the way. Saliva splattered from bared fangs. Hackles raised, bloodshot eyes locked on me with pupils fully dilated, vacant of all but rage. I'd never seen a dog so fast before. He was on the street in a blink, howling with desperation for a taste of easy prey.

Slowly, calmly, Kodi placed himself between me and the frighteningly mad hound. Leaning his black bear powerful body on my leg, he looked straight at the rushing dog and released a deep rumble, shaking the ground beneath the entire block. Windows rattled in their frames, mailboxes opened their yawning mouths, car alarms squawked annoyingly. The dog fumbled with terrified paws to halt its forward momentum and fell directly on his chin. Standing, it turned to flee back behind the freshly broken fence with the mewling cry of a newborn pup.

Kodi, tail wagging, gently bounced against my side keeping me rooted to the spot. Those enormous, sweet caramel brown eyes looked at me to make certain I was unharmed. I scratched behind his ear to reassure him, though my heart battered inside my ribcage at a speed ready for hospitalization. He smeared a swath of thick, sticky drool on my thigh and gleefully trotted to sniff out the nearest tree where he lifted his hind leg to pee.

For a few months Kodi didn't like us going out in the backyard. Every time I slid the screen door open, he'd unleash a frightened yelp and shove his body against my legs trying to keep me in the house. I'd hush him and scratch the top of his head. Nothing seemed to calm him down until I went back inside.

That particular night the grass was praying to the moon again while crickets sang their hymns. Shadows of the trees lay long across the ground, the soft warm breeze felt like kisses on my skin. I stood up from my deck chair and rested my beer bottle on the armrest. Arms stretched over my head, I could feel the knots creak and pull to a welcomed release along my spine. Looking out over the lawn, I couldn't see Kodi at first. I blew out a short whistle and he came trotting towards me from around the corner of the house.

"There's my boy." He was so tall that I didn't need to bend over to give him a few pats on the head. He rubbed against my leg with enough force to knock me off balance leaving a string of sticky drool on my new sweatpants. "Aw shit...not a Newfie hug man! I just got these!" Pushing him away I brushed at the wet spot only making it worse and getting my hands gross in the process. Michelle giggled from her spot on the couch in the living room. "Thanks a lot, babe."

"My pleasure!" She said and went back to her Newsweek article about Hilary Clinton or some other politician I wasn't interested in.

Kodi's hair stood up on the back of his neck. He groaned nervously stalking slowly to the edge of the trees to sniff out the bothersome fox or squirrel, and I turned to head in for a wet towel to clean up. Reaching for the door, a reflection of motion caught the corner of my eye. Kodi was barking at something and I thought I heard Michelle say my name. Then my head detonated in an agonizing flash of searing white light and I didn't hear anything anymore.

A muffled crackle of rustling leaves shuffled low at the edge of my ears. My stomach twisted in knots, and my recently swallowed beer violently attempted to shove its way back up my throat onto the wooden planks of our deck. Snapping leaves and breaking twigs grew louder. Barking and a low growl seeped in and out of the mix.

Thud. Thud. Thud... pounded in quick succession followed immediately by the muffled sounds of a woman's screaming voice. "Mark? Mark! Oh God Mark!" My arms were numb, my eyes unable to open. White blinding pain shot through the back of my skull. I surrendered and submerged into the welcoming darkness once again.

The barking grew louder, and directly on top of me. What felt like leaves and branches ripped at my clothes and searched inside my skin for a firmer grasp. My eyelids were heavy as concrete slabs, and no matter how hard I struggled to see, the muscles hadn't strength enough to raise them. I tried pushing myself up, but I couldn't feel my arms. Again, my head burned and I was submerged helpless into the black.

A million soft, small, fur-like brushes brushed against what skin I had left that was not already ragged and torn. The growling roared on top of my head now. Kodi stood above me chewing and tearing at whatever latched on sucking the life away from me. With every bite he took the thing tightened its grip and pushed out a little more life sustaining air from my lungs. It wasn't human. It was much rougher and harder than any person's arms. Dry leaves cracked as Kodi bit through them to get to the meat of my attacker.

Ribs snapped one by one as the fight intensified. I pulled and clawed for air with every cell in my being, quickly losing the ability to remain conscious. Michelle's voice screeched from the protective safety of the house. I prayed it was safe anyway. Kodi wrestled and tugged at my restraints even harder as I felt myself fading away one last time.

The big dog howled and roared. His dreadful sounds of fear and pain knifed my heart. He sounded so...human. As if he was screaming "No! I won't let you take him!"

A shattering crunch was followed by all encompassing release. I pulled in at the air like I had never breathed oxygen before. Dizziness came in waves while I struggled to hold my weight with my hands. Orange, red and brown leaves covered the deck in abstract. Mixed in were wet patches of a thick golden brown and some splatters of dark crimson. I smelled blood and syrup. Vampire pancake is the first thought I remember floating through my incoherent brain.

Then Kodi howled. I tried to turn my head, but my neck didn't move. I concentrated every muscle I could find and forced myself to roll over. A sharp pain pierced my lower right side. The tip of something sharp pushed the skin up from the inside of my ribcage, not coming through all of the way. I heard a scream echoing off the walls of the house and out over the moonlit trees. At first I couldn't tell where it was coming from it bounced around so much. Then my chest heaved in for more air and the screams halted.

My eyes opened. A black shape was violently hoisted into the air by a tangle of vines or branches. Leaves and fur flew in every direction. Kodi's jaw sank his brilliant teeth deep into the vine-something and a thick golden brown splattered all over him. White-hot rail ties hammered into my ears at the thrashing flooding toward me. Kodi flipped in the air like a rag doll, and a tearing sound that I will never forget preceded a whimper and thud as his great big black body slammed hard to the ground.

The tall, chewed-up leafless beast rose high over Kodi. Black and grey extensions resembled the vague shape of arms and claws rather than branches. It moved in such a way that my eyes couldn't focus on any details. Ancient and malevolent, I still have no idea where it came from or why it was there. With no eyes, it looked down at me and every muscle in my body burned and trembled. If fear and pain were death, then I was certainly dying. I screamed and prayed to a God I never spoke with before to make it stop.

The burning melted away as the giant turned and leaned over Kodi. The dog lay there motionless on the ground, bleeding from the gaping wound where his left hind leg used to be. The beast watched him for a moment and then the tremors came. Leaves fell almost covering Kodi completely. It lifted his red and black matted leg up high in the air, a trophy. The ground shook as a great wail filled the entire world. I couldn't move. I couldn't breathe. If it came after me again it could surely kill me easily.

"Michelle," I whispered to her image floating by on the insides of my eyelids. Then dark.

Most of my weight went down on the cane. I pushed open the boarded up door and limped gingerly out to the porch. I hadn't been to the house in almost eighteen months, and I probably shouldn't have been back at all. If not for the small army of muscle bound men that we hired to pack our things I would have stayed away. They were all over the place literally throwing everything into unmarked cardboard boxes, stripping them closed with brown packing tape and then humping them quickly down the drive to the moving truck idling in wait, ready to head off to Providence. We were getting the fuck out of Dodge, and how.

The bulge of the revolver in my jacket pocket gave me small comfort. I hated guns and didn't want to bring it with me, but Michelle wouldn't let me go back to the house without it. She couldn't come herself, and I didn't blame her. If it were for any other reason than what my therapist called some sort of "closure," I would have stayed away forever as well.

The stitches on my neck and legs were still sore. I fought the urge to scratch them. The less I fussed with the wounds, the sooner they would heal. That's what the doctors said anyway. There were some aches and pains in my chest where my ribs had broke, nothing that the occasional dose of morphine or slug of whiskey couldn't take care of. My leg would never fully recover though. Michelle fought them to let me keep my foot while I was in surgery. She knew that I would have wanted to remain whole and intact. Even if I would never feel anything from the left knee down again, she made sure they kept me all together.

My breath stuttered out through gritting teeth. If I weren't grinding them together like a dentist's worst nightmare they would have been slamming together cracking in a drumline cadence. This was my first and likely last time there since everything happened. Though the sun climbed high in the sky and a full house of twenty virile, muscular young men who were instructed to race to my side at the slightest whimper, I felt more vulnerable than a baby seal with the bat on its way down for the slaughter.

Every sound made me jump. The wind blew and I almost broke the plate glass window that led to the kitchen by backing into it. A twig snapped and I would have sworn it was my heart exploding inside my chest. My eyes and ears played tricks on me. Every tree's shadow grew longer and reached impossibly long fingers along the grass to drag me into the woods and finish their job that was so rudely interrupted a few short months earlier.

I shook my head listening to one of the moving boys laughing. He probably found my porn stash. A few Playboys and some DVD's, but nothing kinky or too depraved. "You can keep those." I whispered to myself and tried to shrug some of the kinks from my shoulders. Not quite used to walking with a cane yet, I wasn't sure if it was too short, but maybe I'd get it adjusted.

A door slammed and the reflection of the trees warbled in the windows' vibrations. A funhouse mirror, I didn't think I could be more freaked out by those damn trees, but I was wrong. Then I heard it.

It was low and hushed. Part of the wind? I knew it wasn't.

BARK

The guttural call came not from the air, but the ground.

BARK

The house dissolved into the background like a mixing engineer slowly lowering the fader.

MBARK

My eyes narrowed to slits. Suddenly dark, colors dissipated from everything around me.

MMMBARK

Leaves fell from the trees like stones pulled to the center of the grass field in a spiral.

MMMMMMBARK

In an impossible fluid motion, the leaves held still and spiraled at the same time. Weaving in a spinning vertigo my hand opened and the cane silently fell to the ground.

MMMMMMMMMBARK

The ground moved quickly to meet my face tumbling from the patio.

MARK

Everything stopped.

A large black blur sat in the center of the spiral.

Silence...

Stillness...

Kodi's giant black eyes held me in defiance of gravity.
He stood proudly with four legs. My vision blurred and he sat beside me with his head beneath my left hand to support my weight. Warm, his fur clean and soft. His tremendous lungs expanded breathing in deeply through his open mouth.
I looked down longingly at the dog that saved my life. I wanted so badly to thank him. To tell him how much he meant to me. In the months I spent in recovery, even with the nerves shot in my leg, the one wound I knew they would never be able to heal was the big Kodi shaped hole no stitches or surgery could mend.
He didn't turn his head, but his eyes turned to me and I could swear he smiled. I lost balance as his weight pushed into my side and he rested his front paw on my foot. I took in a swift intake of breath feeling the shoe digging into my toes. Not painful, just a reassuring pressure.
"We're almost done." A voice came from the doorway behind me. "Are you ready sir?"

My cane in hand, the empty grass rolling in the wind. I blinked to shake the fog out of my brain.

"Sir?" One of the movers stepped out on to the patio and put his callused hand on my shoulder. "Are you okay sir?"

"Uh... Yeah." My numb voice, the only sound I could muster at the moment. "Whenever you need me..." I turned back to the house to limp my way inside.

"You have some dirt on your shoe sir." He pointed and ran off to help one of his smaller partners carry a box down the stairs.

I wear a special shoe to keep the circulation flowing in my otherwise deadened limb. It has a very thick rubber sole and the top is made of soft, skin-like black leather. I grabbed a paper towel off the counter and leaned down to clean it off. The towel fell to the floor not touching the shoe. Since I knew that I would have to wear it every day, I paid extra for the dirt resistant coating. I don't think I'll be calling any time soon to complain about the paw print.

A CHORUS
OF WOLVES

NEW MOON

"BEGINNING"

LOWELL STRETCHES HIS LONG, POWERFUL MUSCLES. Still dark outside he feels no need to rush. Besides, lounging here is so peaceful in the after. The bed is soft and warm. Lingering scents of detergent chemicals form a small barrier around the bed sheets, but everything else is simply perfect.

"Whoever invented the pillow deserves all the money in the world." Danika purrs without a hint of sarcasm.

"Mmm." He moans, enjoying the tickling sensation of her fingers drawing circles across his freckled and scarred chest. "I'm glad you like."

"I need to eat something. You want?" Nothing but the outline of her soft curves visible in the shadows, she slides to the floor leaving the blanket crumpled at the foot of the bed.

"I do want." His brilliant, pale teeth shimmer through the darkness. "But not food." Thick curtains block most of the city's intrusion, the penthouse loft remaining dim enough for sleep. Her bare feet pad gently over a chilly, recently polished marble floor. Lowell judges time by the depth of shadows and angles of starlight in the available portions of the window. "Pour me a small glass of that Phelan Ivalio on top of the fridge."

With a low-pitched thuck, the cork slides from the neck of the bottle. Citrus and other vine ripened scents mix with her sex, instantly rushing across the long room to his sensitive nose. Interlacing fingers behind his head, he watches her shape search the open kitchen. Pale skin punctuates through the darkness offering lovely glimpses of her lower back and a thigh stretched just beyond the kitchen island's edge. The tall bottle clinks over the rims of two glasses as she fills each with thick, dark liquid. In the dark, the shades of deep scarlet turn black, sloshing beneath the blanket of night's obscurity.

Reaching high to replace the bottle, the curve of her soft breast flattens, pressed against the refrigerator door. She takes a handful of grapes from the counter top and places them in a large bowl along with three enormous strawberries and an unpeeled banana.

"Thank you... my morning star." Hints of a dark baritone vibrate through the lowest border of his whisper. He opens his mouth allowing Danika to insert a large, rugby ball shaped grape. His tongue slides along her finger's length before biting through the fruit's outer flesh. "I do believe you are more ripened than the produce."

"Oh, really?" She teases. Peeling the banana suggestively, she looks down over his firm excitement rising in the darkness. "I don't know about you mister flattery, but I'm going to need at least a few bites of this before we go for round three."

"Take your time beautiful. I'll wait and watch." Lowell turns to the window, his long face split top to bottom by the curtain's lengthy shadow. "For now."

WANING CRESCENT

"IMMERSION"

"IT IS STILL EARLY SIR." The old man stands next to the bed with his master. Crumbling, fragile, his ancient voice trembles beneath the weight of too many years. "There is time to try again."

A warm hand firmly presses against the woman's belly. Lowell's fingers swirl slowly in opposing directions. Searching... Seeking...

"No Zev." Danika wakes to his familiar low-pitched growl. "They are here. I can feel them already." His lips press gently around her pierced bellybutton. She pulls away from the tingle of his breath against moist skin where his skillful tongue orbits in circles. Lowell stands, towering over her prone body. "Unfortunately, I must prepare."

"Of course, sir." Zev lifts her hand pushing his dry, wrinkled finger against the underside of her wrist. He huffs twice. A small, round patch of cold metal touches the skin over her heart. He holds it there, then moves it to another spot above her left breast. It moves again and again around her belly.

"I may have done it this time Zev." Excited as a child seeing Christmas presents from the top of the stairs that first moment under the tree.

"We cannot trust to hope sir." The old hands slide the blanket up to her neck, covering her from the cold air. "We will not know for certain until I can perform a few more tests..."

"I know. I know," Bursting with energy, Lowell presses at the old man. "But what do you *think*? I will not be here for your tests. I need you to *tell* me."

Years of attempts with women brought home from bars, concerts and the occasional informed volunteer. Dozens of sacrifices, failed before reaching the one desired outcome, their mutilated bodies requiring messy disposal, a fortune in payoffs to law enforcement and corrupt political officials.

"How much longer will this go on?" Lowell stalked across the room, arms flailing with frustration.

"She has potential." Zev's shaky hand brushes a stray hair from her damp forehead. "They might survive this time."

A sharp sting enters the soft inner skin of her left elbow. Out of reflex, she pulls at the arm feeling resistance against her wrist. Her other arm is similarly unable to move. Before Danika's brain can send a signal all the way down to lift her legs, the fingers of sleep irresistibly tug her eyelids closed. She dreams of running through tall grass, sinking teeth into fleeing prey's muscle and bone, the bitter tang of fresh blood on the back of her tongue.

LAST QUARTER

"CONTEMPLATION"

LIKE A PAPER BAG WRAPPED OVER an oddly formed miniature watermelon, the wrinkled folds of skin on Zev's face appear to weave through the room buoyed on a blurry cloud of white. Floating across beeping monitor screens, he carries one clear plastic bag filled with thick, dark liquid. He flicks at its side with a finger after hanging it from a sharp hook, high on an extended metal pole. Another hand appears above the white cotton, twisting a small lever that attaches the bottom of the bag to a plastic tube. Flooding the tube, the liquid transfers into the needle taped in place on Danika's forearm.

"You are awake? Good." The old man shines a pen light into her eyes. She squints into the retina burning shine. "How do you feel?"

"Urgh..." her tongue coated with sandpaper refuses to bend and stretch in order to properly form recognizable syllables. He places the straw from a paper cup between her lips. The cold water instantly moistening her mouth washes the sandpaper gristle from her throat. Growing more accustomed to the bright surroundings, Danika loudly gulps another swallow. "Where am I?"

"Please, do not worry yourself. Everything looks perfect Danika my dear." The old man pierces a needle into the side of the rubber tube slowly depressing the syringe. The freshly emptied syringe wobbling from the side of his hand, he holds up three fingers together in front of the shadowy crevasses of his face, "Scout's honor."

"Please...Zev...let me go. I won't tell anyone anything." Words choke out through her swelling throat. "I want to go home. Please just let me go home."

"Come, come my dear." The old man dips his hand into his left lab coat pocket removing a large ring covered in dozens of brass keys. "Enough with such gloominess." Without looking, the old man smoothly inserts a key into the restraint holding her right hand. With a swift twist and soft click, her arm is free. "Why, you should be over the moon! Lowell presented these gifts to a myriad of others without one of them providing such a clean, healthy passage."

"What gifts?" She fights every urge to strike out at the old man with her freed hand. Tugging on the restraint holding her other wrist against the bed, "Passage for what? What exactly is there to be *happy* about?" She flinches at a slow, horrible scraping sound retching through her ears. The heavy metallic chair drags slowly, legs scraping violently across the room until finally coming to rest next to the bed and putting an end to the chalkboard fingernail-like screeches, swathing the room with a thick, nauseating quiet. With nothing but the pulse of blood flowing through her veins, the old man arrives at her side taking his seat.

"Indeed." Every syllable leaves his lips with a calm, deliberate intention. He doesn't appear rehearsed, although she has the idea that similar conversations have taken place many times in this room. "While understanding your concern," his pale eyes hold for a beat on the restraints, "I really must impress upon you the honor you should feel at being chosen."

"So I should be privileged that you strapped me down like an animal?" She slides a finger under the cuff, pulling. "Let me go."

"My dear, these restraints are here for your protection." Zev's smile exposes his yellowed, smoker teeth. "You must remain here until the passage is complete."

Is the room moving?

Are they on a ship of some kind?

"Where are you taking me?"

The old man chuckles and pats her thigh. "You are not going anywhere my dear. It will all be over soon. Then Danika, you are free to go, if you still choose to leave us of course."

"You sadistic prick." Venom seethes between the vowels.

"Ours have searched for countless years to find a mate with the proper balance." His sickly teeth, made more prominent by the pale lab coat, grin between blue-tinged, vibrating lips.

"What the hell are you talking about?" Her free hand snatches for his face. With inhuman speed, the old man is beyond her reach. He is nothing but the white blur of his lab coat and the glint reflecting from his graying widow's peak. In a blink, Zev is standing at the foot of the bed, coattail flapping gently in the breeze created by his escape from her attack. "How the..." Intending to rip the IV out, Danika feels the cuff holding her arm down once more.

"As I mentioned earlier Danika, the restraints are here for your protection."

WANING GIBBOUS

"CO-OPERATION"

WITH NO WINDOWS, light bulbs or other visible source of illumination, a constant haze of grays and whites drifts through the room. Aided by unknown heavy medication, the heart monitor's beeping is a meditative mantra lulling Danika's senses. When thoughts coalesce tightly enough for her to conceptualize an escape, more of the drug drips through the IV to scatter them away like pheasants fleeing the sound of a shotgun.

Cold hands touch her skin. Fingers press firmly against her wrist and throat. Her thighs are spread apart as the foot of the bed falls away leaving her feet elevated and separated by padded stirrups. A small curtain blocks the sight of anything beyond the top of her breasts.

"What are you doing?" An unfamiliar pressure settles over her entire body from the stomach down. "I can't feel my legs."

"Mmm?" Zev's familiar wrinkles peek over the sheet. "Oh, yes. We don't want you to feel any discomfort my dear." He disappears behind the white barrier again. "This will only take a few moments... longer...and now...we...are..."

His back crooked and bent, Zev stands with a tired moan. His gloved hand leaves bloody fingerprints on the sheet as he pulls it down to cover her legs. Stealing her breath, reality brass knuckles punch deep into her thoughts. She pulls at the restraints, digging dark red welts into her skin, knowing full well they are too strong to break. Alarmed by the crack of metal clanging as surgical tools fall against the tray, Danika whips her head to the left. Noticing her attention shift to his hands, Zev fumbles to cover the freshly used, moist blades and forceps with a smudged towel.

Her eyes fiercely squash to avoid the sight. Though medication provides a barricade from the physical pain of whatever horrifying surgeries the old man is performing, panic drives nightmare images in her mind of what malicious practices those sharp tools are undertaking below the sheet. The scream comes from deep within. Danika's arms thrash banging her head into the bed, shoulders thrusting side to side. Bolt. Flee. Escape.

"Hush now. Everything is progressing quite well my dear." Zev wipes his hands on a black towel. "Lowell will be extremely unhappy if you hurt yourself or..." Danika cannot help but see his hunger for the hidden parts of her below the sheet.

"What did you do to me?" Her voice came as a primal growl unburdened by fear, but on the precipice of brutal eruption.

"It was necessary to make room." His lab coat sleeve absorbs sweat from his brow. "Your body, beautiful as it is, was simply not large enough to accommodate the passage." His hands press palm to palm and slowly pull apart to shoulder width as a visual aid. "Danika, I promise you are being well tended to. Scout's honor."

Zev pushes more drugs into the IV. Straining to reject it back through the needle, her muscles flex to close herself from the deadening effects. Clouds swell in a gentle, grey circle around her eyes. Everything feels soft and gentle. Drowning, she has no choice but to relent to the bonds of numbness, her screams resolve to the whimper of a whipped dog. Nebulous images wash over the ceiling, showing a tall man with dark golden eyes and whips of thin black hair covering his tail.

FULL MOON

"CULMINATION"

"I'VE WARMED IT FOR YOU MY DEAR. Please relax." With long, spindly fingers Zev squeezes clear green gel from a plastic bottle above Danika's recently popped belly button. It peeked out along with the feeling of the first strong kicks. "Let us see now, here."

The click of a keyboard stroke sounds and the printer whirs. She sees one fleeting glimpse of blurred image before the paper curls, falling into the receiving tray. The room warbles and turns to double. But not from medication. Tears form a thin layer and drain into her silently screaming open mouth. Her head turns into the pillow burrowing away to nothingness.

"Sir," Zev speaks into a telephone attached to the sonogram machine's table. "It is almost time. Yes sir. No, I do not believe so. Would you like me to... Yes sir, I await your arrival."

"We should clean you up my dear." Zev removes a moist towel from the box beneath the machine and wipes the gel from her belly. "Lowell is on his way. He is most excited." Too depleted of strength to resist, she wishes for the ability to retreat deep into her mind, to escape. She thinks about disappearing into a beautiful fantasy of soft kisses and strawberry wine. Powerful arms laying her on a soft bed covered in silk-sheeted pillows. Thousands of candles standing in perfect rows until they vanish in the distance. A piano sings a melody written for no one but her. He leans over her. He leans against her. He leans into her. *"My morning star."* Lowell...

A door flies open and Zev straightens his crook of a back as far as he can. No matter how far he tries, he still resembles a living question mark. Like a whisper, a thin shadow shivers, pulling all the light into its dense gravity traversing the room.

Despite the powerful will not to look, she is pulled in by Lowell's charisma. Her nose alert and attentive, finds fragrances from collective memories buried deep in the recesses of human experience.

Here is the winter forest...
Here is moist snow on the ground between tall leafless, black trees...
Here is a trail of enormous, stalking footprints...
Here is tracking, pursuing...
Here is the hunt...
Here is the shadow...
Here is blood...

"Zev," Lowell's deep, familiar voice soothes and climbs the walls surrounding her frightened heart despite all of its jagged battlements.

"Good evening Lowell." Zev nods his head in a subtle unmistakable bow of subservience. "Welcome home."

"Thank you." Lowell reaches to gently stroke the shape of Danika's toe through the thick sheets. His touch sends a charged bolt across her body. "Show me."

"Yes sir." Zev pulls pages of paper from the printer tray. "They are healthy."

"And, the passage?" Lowell speaks in a cracked whisper. For the first time, Danika hears panic in his voice.

"They should be descending very soon sir."

"I can't believe..." He grips the old man's upper arms tightly. "Is it really true?"

Danika can't focus on any definition in their faces. A sickly green glow soaks the old man's beard. It pulsates, absorbing the Frankenstein hue swimming along the flickering screen. Lowell grins, the corners of his mouth open wide, stretching back. Cheeks tearing from lip to ear, his teeth were now a treacherous landscape, jagged and sharp, built for ripping, tearing and shredding. The bone-shattering grin turns to face Danika. A long, black tongue bobbles with his lungs in shallow, quick pants. One droplet of misty drool hangs from the tip, moments from dropping through the air. Then his face is beautiful and magnificent, human again.

"Isn't this exciting?" Lowell shakes with anticipation.

Under the scream, bile climbs Danika's throat. It begins as a shrill, glass-vibrating shriek, before drowning below a congested gag. Small, partially digested lumps of her previous evening's meal swim in a semi-transparent liquid haze. Her body writhes, eyes roll back to full white in seizure.

"Zev!" Lowell sucks in a deep breath lunging to support her head.

"She does not remember." Rifling through an open drawer full of medicines, one small bottle is thrown over the edge shattering to the floor. The hard sole of his shoe crackles atop broken glass. Zev gasps, finding what he needs.

"Is that possible?" Despite steeled, powerful muscles, Lowell is pulled down. Danika's sweat-covered forehead smashes into his pinnacle angled Roman nose collapsing it sideways, broken and blooded. Fingers open reflexively to cover his face falling backward on the floor.

Zev strips the cap from a syringe, his mouth spits the plastic across the room. With trembling hands, he fills it completely with a brown, syrupy fluid. The needle enters Danika's vein deep inside her inner elbow. The plunger is depressed pushing its entire contents into her spastic body.

"There." Within seconds the thrashing subsides. Danika breathes slowly, peacefully. Zev falls to his knees. "Sir, are you alright?"

"Other than my broken nose?" Lowell leans forward palming the floor. Blood oozes between clenched fingers, his once perfectly featured face, now has a smashed crooked relic of flesh engorging from the center. The skin around his eyes is visibly turning blackish purple, bruised. "What do you mean she doesn't remember? How can she not remember?"

"Perhaps it is part of the passage." Zev slowly pulls himself to his feet using the side of the bed. "It could be a part of why she is our first successful vessel."

"But how can she forget who she is?" Lowell takes the black towel from Zev's hand, gingerly holding it to his crushed nose. "Our morning star."

"Yes. But no one has come this far before. We simply do not completely understand the chemical reactions occurring in her body." Zev steps over the broken glass and shivers. He presses his fingers to her neck and looks at his watch.

"We shouldn't have done this." Lowell kicks the wall with his pointed boot leaving a small, dark hole in the otherwise smooth white. "I knew it would turn bad."

"Now sir, you know we had no choice." The old man places a shriveled hand on the shoulder of Lowell's once perfectly pressed and tailored suit. "We mustn't disturb her rest any further. Her condition continues to be rather fragile. I hope we have not caused irreparable damage already."

"Yes," Lowell nods and backs away from the monitor holding a towel to his face. "Of course."

"May I?" Raspy and thin, Danika's voice emerges from the ether. Dumbfounded, the two men look at one another unsure of what to do. "Please? I want to see."

"Sir?" Zev looks to his master with palms up and shrugs. Lowell's nod is all but imperceptible, his expression drifting between anxiety and joy. The old man turns the table holding the ultrasound machine. Wheels creak, wires and cables must be moved in order to free up space for the turn.

Danika stares at the display's glowing, pale lime image. Near indecipherable, thick black spaces intersperse with unstable green lines. Her eyes strain for any sign of recognizable shapes until something moves. A leg? A hand? The face...is that a face? It's long, too long. Another uncurls from behind. She finds a third and then a much smaller fourth in the background.

"You see my dear?" Zev nods his head reassuringly.

"What...what?" Danika feels the sting of another needle prick into her arm. "What is this?" Chemical sleep wraps its warm fingers across her eyes putting to rest any confusion or fear.

WAXING GIBBOUS

"ASSESSMENT"

SILENTLY SHE PURSUES HER ENEMY. The thief spinelessly crept in the night stealing one of her helpless young into the lightless, freezing darkness. Leaves of grass bow silently beneath her swift feet. Long ears lift high, probing for any sound out of place. Using her formidable nose, she discovers traces of squirrels, field mice, ants... everything that passed this way. The faintest trace from her young one confirms that she is indeed tracking close behind.

There. Behind that thicket of trees she spots him. The pure white of his coat shines through the branches, a beacon. Making no effort to camouflage may well be his undoing. She moves through the brush, over fallen twigs and stones, quiet as a gentle breath. A few more steps and she will be upon him. The old man reveals no sign he knows she is near.

Two steps away and the trap springs. A rope tightens around her calf, flung high into the air, her body spins in slow circles above the ground. She howls in pain from the thought of her family now left motherless and alone. The old man turns, cradling a small bundle wrapped in a black blanket with an odd pattern of reflective, moist splotches.

"Hush my dear. There is no need for tears." The old man tickles his fingers behind her ear. "All we desire is to ensure the safety of your children. Everything will be well." He holds up three fingers of his right hand. "Scouts honor."

She wants to scream. She wants to curse him to the high heavens. She wants to call for help from anyone who might hear. A sound rises from deep within her chest exploding from between her newfound sharp teeth. The ground shakes. The rope bursts. She falls, landing solidly on four paws. Jaws snap at the blanket, teeth rip it from the old man's grasp revealing pallid fur matted in clumps over pale, nearly transparent skin covered in maps of winding black veins. She licks the young one's limp face, willing life to return.

The old man stands firm with no fear, smiling confidently. Foolish. Her terrifying jaws rip into his throat tearing his head from its body. His colorless hair collects stones and twigs while tumbling along the ground. His body remains upright defiantly holding the lifeless child in his arms. She rises on hind legs falling forward to drive her teeth into the blood-spattered shoulder.

FIRST QUARTER

"ACTION"

DANIKA WAKES UNDER FRESHLY WARMED BLANKETS. Her belly rises in the mound of soft white sheets. Mounds bulging from within, the offspring stretch their muscles to prepare for passage into the world. She lays her head back on the soft, down pillow closing her eyes trying to forget what is coming.

Long, powerful fingers gently entwine with her hand. In the shadows, Lowell sits at her bedside with his head bowed low.

"Lowell." Barely a whisper escapes her lips.

"Yes morning star. I am here." Pressing his lips to her wrist, the wetness of a tear trails down her skin and on to the bed sheet.

"Please let me go."

"I cannot until the passage is complete." He releases her hand. His eyes are damp, lips trembling. He appears genuinely sad.

"You keep saying that." Louder, her voice echoes from the hard cold walls. "You and Zev. You're like fucking machines set on repeat. Why won't you tell me what it is?"

Lowell stands, walking slowly to the foot of her bed. "Unfortunately your memory has been affected by the process. You are not a prisoner my dear. You came here with us voluntarily."

"I doubt that."

"Never the less, it is the truth." Lowell places his hands on her ankles. She twists and writhes until he releases her, holding his arms out in a gesture of peace.

"I found you several months ago." He slips his hands into the deep pockets of his coat. "We were both attending a fundraiser at Roger Williams Park to raise money for the homeless."

"People who won't be missed." Danika growled low and spiteful. "Don't you eat them for midnight snacks?"

Lowell laughs. "There are times when we find our sustenance in the darkened alleyways of Providence. But it is not common." Tapping his finger on the bedside table he scratched his chin with the other hand. "I do have a conscience despite appearances. I wish to help even the most pitiful of creatures climb their way out of the gutter to better lives."

"Whatever." Under her breath, she turns her head away from him. "Just because we met at a party doesn't give you the right to rape and kidnap me."

"I apologize if that is the impression you have." He sits down in the chair and places his hand gently on the edge of the mattress, careful not to touch her. "Once I conveyed to you the story of my people, you became more than willing to help."

"Did you drug me?"

"Absolutely not." Lowell pulls up to protest. "We were together."

"I seriously doubt that asshole."

"We are in love." Lowell shifts his gaze to an emptiness somewhere deep beneath the floor.

"Then why don't I remember?" Danika lifts the pitch of her voice, feeling a tug in the center of her chest.

"The process changes you."

"Are you talking about this?" She looks at the large curve of her belly. Lowell nods.

"Yes. Let me tell you who we are." Lowell leans against the backrest of the chair releasing a long, slow breath. Resting his head on outstretched fingertips, he speaks deliberate and hushed. "The myth of my kind's condition being contagious runs rampant. Doubtless you have heard the insatiable fairy tales. Nonsense. A mere scratch or nibble will not gift a creature so flimsy as a human with our magnitude. Perhaps the rumors began when some poor villager discovered a victim's remains. We often hunt in packs, so it stands to reason that more casualties would be found nearby."

Lowell scratches his chin, eyes flashing a deep red burning ferociously in the dim light. "Fear penetrates the fragile veil of sanity so very easily. Running themselves in childish circles, the villagers most likely snatched some poor soul whose behavior disconcerted their limited sensibilities, cast blame for every fowl occurrence and created their *Monster!*"

Danika shudders at the pleasure Lowell seems to take from people's terror. *How could I possibly love this beast?* Thoughts of escape continue their run through the plains of her mind.

"Rather than accept the terrifying possibility that they were not indeed the pinnacle of all God's creatures, they clung to their arrogance. As a balm for their nightmares they continued to manufacture fiendish beasts, shape shifters, blood feasters and vengeful spirits from beyond the grave. These provided but a small morsel of understanding to placate the masses while sucking thumbs beneath their blankets in the dark."

"How do you explain the myths here in America?" Danika pulls back at his touch.

"Rumors fly much faster than hunting eagles my dear." Lowell raises an eyebrow as if speaking to a child. "They cannot be stopped. Alas, we are few. We have always been few. Never more than a handful of our kind exist at one time. We live primarily in the company of our own. We love and have families. And after what humans would consider an unnaturally long life we do in fact die."

He walks slowly to the dresser on the other end of the room and pours a glass of water. Taking a sip, he holds it up in offer to Danika. She shakes her head.

"Go on. Please." As he speaks, the walls tumble brick by slow brick in her mind. Images of a gentle caress, soft butterfly kissing and his body wrapped around her from behind through the night begin to appear.

"Our species hangs on the precipice of extinction. We may no longer be able to extend our lineage through the expanse of time." His deep voice cracks revealing the deeply dug well of pain tunneling through him. "The majority of my people are not as blessed with the gift of agelessness as I. Most are dying if not dead. If we do not breed, we will vanish."

The salt of a tear crawls in between her pursed lips. She licks it away and lifts her shoulder against her cheek to catch more as they fall.

"We are losing our women. There have only been three known female births in four centuries." He holds up three fingers to emphasize the lonely point. "The first was shot to death during the beginning of the Nine Years War in Ireland. With her Pequot village overrun by colonists in Narragansett, our second girl died of exposure. Much as it pains me to recall aloud, my own wife and daughter died during childbirth. That is all. We are nearing our end."

"I'm so sorry Lowell." Danika, remembering the months spent together, how he cared for her, how they worked together to bring a future to his people, finds her muscles releasing.

"A flaw hidden deep within our genome, only recently discovered by Zev, has mutated to the point where we can no longer produce female offspring." Lowell resumes his seat holding her hand, squeezing gently. "For more than one hundred years Zev and I have attempted to create a new, pure generation. In countless countries we scoured the world for a human woman who could survive the passage. Their fragile bodies simply could not withstand the demands our gestation period placed upon them. All of our attempts have failed. Until now. Until you."

WAXING CRESCENT

"GROWING"

DANIKA'S CHILDREN MOVE SAFELY through her passage. She can taste their scent now. Waking this morning, everything emerged clear and distinct beyond the fog. Despite Lowell's objections she knew this would work. Regaining herself, her purpose, no other could provide safety to the line, only she.

SUITE SWEET

"There is a devil in every berry of the grape."

—THE KORAN

YOU COULD FIND IT BURIED DEEP under the brown smoggy haze of the northern San Fernando Valley, hidden in a strip mall along with the remnants of a Blockbuster Video and the long-closed Alpha Beta super market. In between the failed Korean nail salon and a mom-and-pop pharmacy with dust-covered shelves stood The Suite Sweet. The worst bar in Los Angeles, California.

The dark atmosphere wasn't created by candlelight or electronic dimming switches. No, there were five 50-watt bulbs in the entire place dangling from exposed wire. Two of them drooped low from the ceiling over the back bar. More often than not, what little illumination they shed was disorienting due to the bartender bumping into them while he reached for bottles of gin, cheap watered down whiskey and other bland cocktail ingredients. One bulb burned and popped directly in the center of the room, its cracked and chipped faux Tiffany shade cast an asymmetrical pattern across stained and sticky yellow shag carpeting. Of the remaining two, you would find one in the damp unisex bathroom in the back, while the other drifted useless, broken and unchanged just inside the warped and weathered front door.

When the state passed their non-smoking laws, the Suite Sweet either chose to boldly ignore the legislation and risk heavy fines, or it simply paid no attention to the matter whatsoever. Thick blankets of deep brown perpetually hung high to the ceiling from cheap cigars, while Pall Malls and Diplomat butts filled the tin ash trays placed on the bar and the four semicircular booth tables along the far wall. Newcomers desperately rummaged for a clean breath as their lungs seized, quivered and quickly choked the moment they first stepped inside.

When Kirsten acted on her threats and finally kicked him out, the Suite Sweet was where Trevor eventually ended up. He blamed it on her immature insecurities. Though he did forget to erase his browser's history showing visits to an absurdly long list of porn and dating sites that she eventually found on their computer. Whatever the case might have been, his childhood bedroom with the same faded Star Wars bed sheets was now his resting place. Having to deal with mom's nagging and dad's passive aggressiveness should've been enough punishment, but the "no alcohol under our roof" policy was more than he could handle at that particular moment.

Back in the day, he and his buddies passed by the Suite Sweet more times than he could remember. The bar was a local fixture that squatted in the same spot for decades. In high school they used to sit in the parking lot pounding beers in their cars before football games or parties. They'd hear the crappy old music leaking through the door and taste the smell of stale and rotting pickles. Even with all the double-dog dares and teasing, nobody they ever knew actually dared go inside.

The story usually spread around after a few drinks and bong hits at parties. Billy Dean, the best running back Kennedy Cougars had ever seen, refused to back down on a dare from his quarterback Marshall Thomas. His rep would never recover from something like that.

"I dare you to go in, slap a twenty on the bar and order a Slippery Nipple," Marshall shouted in a slur, making sure the couch stayed in place while the room spun around him.

"I spent my last twenty on the beer man." Billy waved him off and threw an empty can across the room.

"Fine. Pussy out man."

"Nah. I'll go. Gimme the money."

"Hey! Who got twenty bucks?" He shouted over the music roaring from the stereo. Hands went around collecting the cash. Fingers pointed and somewhere in another room a glass sculpture of a leaping stallion fell and shattered across the floor.

Money collected, Marshall wagged the bills in Billy's face. "You ain't gonna do it man. You a pussy!"

"Don't think I won't, bitch." Billy stumbled to his fire engine red El Camino, ran through the stop sign and parked diagonally between three spaces in front of the Suite Sweet.

When Billy didn't come back to the party that night, Marshall boasted and crowed that he'd won the bet. Two days later when the El Camino was found in the parking lot of a shopping mall in Valencia, nobody laughed anymore. Billy never came back and the Cougars lost every remaining game that season. Not many people paid attention to the crying old man with empty eyes sitting at the far end of the bleachers.

Trevor finished dinner alone in his room. Once Mom turned on the TV, he quietly sneaked out and drove down the hill to the old parking lot. Most of his friends had moved on to successful lives, at least on the surface. With powerful careers at Fortune 500 companies, Stepford wives and the prerequisite 2.3 children. They probably had dogs and goldfish too. Whatever. Inhaling the discharge of the remaining leaves in his one hitter, he blew bluish smoke out the driver's side window watching the bird nest-filled neon sign alternately flashing Suite and Sweet.

"Okay. Why not?" The Honda's door screeched in the cold air and his flip fops slapped against wet concrete leading him beneath the sign's orange and green glow. As he reached for the rusted cast iron handle, a surge of anxiety flushed his cheeks. Not panic, but an oddly familiar darkness. A primal and instinctive warning that said, "This place just ain't right Trevor boy. Let's get us someplace else huh?"

Perhaps it was the pot masking his gut feelings. Then again it might have been the bitterness of being dumped. More likely it was the unconscious need to do something he knew all those guys living so much better than him never had the guts to do.

The door opened and instantly he was shrouded in smoke. Resisting an urge to reach his hands out and part the hazy curtains, he coughed. The finely coated pipes of Paul Anka crooning "(You're) Having My Baby" swam muffled through the fog. Ice clinked in a glass hidden far away in the darkness of a corner booth to his right.

Next to the jukebox, a man's light tan suit coat flopped over the back of a chair wrinkled and dirty. He leaned on the machine with one hand supporting his weight, eyes closed he mouthed the lyrics out of time with the song. A dark stain coated the back of his trousers, hopefully just a trick of the lights reflected off the mirror that swayed in circles behind the bar.

Trevor stood in between two stools with red cushions looking at the collection of dust-covered bottles. Fixated on the dust-covered illegible labels, he didn't notice the coaster sliding down the length of the black stained mahogany until it hit him in the hand.

"So this gorgeous gal comes in here the other night, right?" The bartender, sitting on a short wooden seat inside the far end of the bar looked up from cleaning a highball glass. "She shimmies right over to the very spot you're standin'." He adjusted his thin rainbow striped suspenders.

"Excuse me?" Trevor looked around finding himself alone at the bar.

"She's all sultry like, wearing a skin tight mini-skirt and cutoff tank top." Using the palm of his hand, the bartender nudged the light bulb away from his head as he stood. Nearly seven feet tall, his long limbs moved more gracefully than one might expect. "I, bein' of a single ready to mingle status, of course drop what I'm doin' and come over to see if I can be of any assistance. She leans over real close like." The bartender came to a stop directly in front of Trevor placing his palms flat on the bar.

"Her finger curls like she's askin' me to lean in too. So I does, right?" He spun his index finger in the long strands of a bushy dark beard. "Then she takes her hand and starts all rubbin' and caressin' my face. Now I'm gettin' all excited you know?"

"Okay." Trevor hoisted himself on the stool to his left, giving the odd scenario a hesitant grin.

"Then she says to me real soft and smoky like, 'Are you the manager?' Well, I ain't so I says 'Sorry ma'am. He ain't here right now.' She starts movin' her fingers through my hair and playin' with my ear. Had the biggest boner of my life right?" The bartender adjusted his crotch and placed a shot glass on the bar in front of himself never breaking eye contact with Trevor.

"Then she says, 'Is there any way you can get him for me? It's real important.'" He raised an unlabeled bottle of clear liquid and filled the shot glass to the brim not spilling a drop. "'Wish I could. Is there anything that I can do for you beautiful?' I says winkin' and grinnin'. 'Yes. Please give him this message.' Then she sticks her fingers in my mouth. In my mouth right? So I start lickin' and suckin' on 'em. It's the best night of my life right?" The bottle swept back under the bar, shot glass in his hand in one swift continuous blur of motion.

"What was the message?" Trevor asked, though not at all sure he wants to know the answer.

"There ain't no toilet paper in the bathroom." He downed the shot without a flinch, slamming the glass into the sink behind the bar. "So what can I get ya my man?"

Trevor blinked through the smoky air, his breath catching shallow in his lungs. Normally very cocksure and strong, he forced another uncomfortable grin. From the shadows at the end of the bar a throaty chuckle, not much more than a cough, rumbled through the smoke toward him. A small red-orange circle glowed brightly and then dimmed along with a flick of ashes falling into the tray in front of the old woman. She bit down on the end of her long, thin cigarette, still laugh-coughing.

"Stop bein' suck a jagoff. Give that boy a whiskey." Her wrinkled, bony claw hoisted a nearly empty rocks glass in his direction.

"Thank you." Trevor nodded politely. The bartender reached under the bar to the well drinks.

"Give him something good Lurch. Come on you cheap bastard. None of that piss water down there." The old lady took a long drag from the cigarette.

"You know I hate it when you call me that Bridgit."

"Well then, I sincerely apologize Artie." Bridgit blew a kiss to the bartender.

"It's okay." Trevor looked over through the haze at the old woman. "I'll drink the well stuff. It's fine."

"Like hell it is!" Spit shoots from her tongue. "Top shelf or piss off."

Artie shook his head bumping into the low hung light, sending long fingers of shadows dancing across the bar. A deep, moist plunk accompanied the cork pulling from the neck of a wide bottle with a red label. "Top shelf. No piss."

"Thanks." Trevor inhaled a deep sniff over the glass, enjoying the twang through his nostrils. "Cheers." Raising his glass, Bridgit followed suit downing the rest of hers in one gulp.

"Don't love me." She cradled the glass in her hands, carefully swirling the remaining ice around in circles. Her voice was soft, barely audible above the music.

"I'm sorry. What?" Trevor looks at Artie who tilted his head in the old lady's direction.

"Don't love me." Unflinching, her gaze bore deep into him, spectral eyes buried in deep sockets sunken by time.

Before Trevor could respond, a loud thump barked from the jukebox and the irritating scrape of a needle across record ridges. Apparently the man in the wrinkled suit decided to sit on the floor next to the machine with his eyes closed to make himself more comfortable. Artie shrugged his shoulders unsurprised by the event.

"Excuse me, Bridgit was it?" Trevor shifted to a stool closer to the end of the bar. "Were you..."

"Shut the fuck up. I love this song." The old woman closed her eyes swaying gently along and humming to Dan Hill's "Sometimes When We Touch".

"Wow." Under his breath, Trevor raised his eyebrows and quickly finished his drink. He took a ten-dollar bill from his wallet and set it on the bar. "Thanks Artie. It's been...well it has certainly been."

"Keep your money." Artie continued cleaning bottles next to the mirror without turning around. "First timers get one free."

"Okay. Thanks." Trevor nodded his head looking at Artie's skeletal thin face in the mirror. "I guess."

"Don't stiffen your nethers pal. Suite Sweet policy." Artie turned around slowly, cleaning rag over his shoulder. "Keeps 'em comin' back."

"Yeah." Trevor lifted an eyebrow at the nearly empty room. "I can see that."

"You want another, you pay for it." Artie pointed to the bottle of Bookers on the top shelf. "You pay for it."

"You know what?" Trevor climbed back on the stool. "Fuck it. Let's get a round for the house." Trevor boosted the empty glass high above his head. Bridgit matched the toast gulping down the majority of her freshened beverage.

"...in love with ...I shoulda'... heart wants what..." The wrinkled suit man grumbled in drunk speak, allowing Artie to assist his movements to the nearest table. "... I didn't listen...not me ..." Muffling more unintelligible sounds muffled by his face buried in the table top.

"Thanks for the drink," Bridgit said, her fingers callused and dry on his forearm. He pulled away quickly, too quickly to be deemed as polite. "Easy now fella. I won't bite." Missing two teeth on the top and another few on the bottom, her yellow smile was more menacing than friendly. Strangely, Trevor found himself a tad bit attracted to her.

"Uh, you're welcome."

"What's your name?"

"Trevor." He stammered. "Trevor Donne."

"I'm gonna call you Caper." She patted him on the arm gently with a nod to the bartender for a refill.

"But my name's..."

"So Caper, ain't been in here before has ya?" Bridgit tapped a thin cigarette out of the Pall Mall box in front of her. Her thick lipstick smeared itself over the long filter while she lit a match and put fire to the end. "What's your sob story?"

"No sob story here."

"I call bullshit on that one." Artie leaned back against the inside corner of the bar. Bridgit's cough-laugh echoed around the dark room. "Nobody comes in this stank den unless they got no place else to go."

"Amen Lurch." She took a long drag from her smoke pointing the cigarette at Trevor. "Spill it Caper." Trevor placed his glass gently down on the coaster, pushed it away and stood. Turning to leave, his progress was prevented by the sound of another barking laugh-cough. "She kicked you out didn't she?"

"Hmm. What a rare and unique situation that a man would go to a bar because of a broken heart." Trevor spun on his heel. "You must be psychic."

"More like psychotic." Artie laughed too high-pitched and girlish for a man of his size.

"I am." Bridgit coughed again, looking at the bartender. "A little bit anyways."

"Right." Moving for the door again, Trevor waved his hand behind his back toward the old lady. "Whatever."

Standing in the damp wind, the door swung slowly behind him. Before it closed, he heard a gravel encrusted voice say, "Caper needs to quit knocking himself off with those skin flicks," followed by a clinking of glasses and throaty laughter.

Staring at the World War II aircraft and spaceship models hanging from the ceiling over his bed, Trevor couldn't stop thinking about her. Overwhelmed with details both hidden and exposed, Bridgit spewed insults through his brain until the glow of sunrise's long nails clawed through the slits between the blinds.

He sat up in bed feeling an unfamiliar stiffness in his back. He stretched, cracks and pops zipping up his spine providing a small hint of relief. Waiting for hot shower water to arrive, he leaned on the sink closing his eyes. The shape in the mirror seemed a bit wider than he was familiar with. Instead of wiping the fog away and closely scrutinizing his image, he slipped beneath the stream of falling water hoping to wash his skin clean of the stale smoke redolence from the Suite Sweet.

"Hey Jules." Calling in sick, he decided to take advantage of some time off before the year ended. "How're things in the pit today?"

"Hi Trevor." His assistant sounded honestly concerned, still eager to make a good impression after two years working together. "I was beginning to worry about you. You didn't answer your home phone or your cell."

"I know. I'm not coming in for the next day or so." Trevor pressed the speaker button on the phone, slipping on a pair of white briefs. "Can you cover for me?"

"Sure, I guess." Jules lowered his voice. "The old man's on a rampage. Pissed off you're not here. What do you want me to tell him?"

"Tell him I'm sick."

"With what? If you're not bleeding out the asshole you're supposed to be here."

"Then I guess I'm bleeding out the ass." Trevor hung up. No point in continuing that conversation. The less Jules knew, the less trouble he'd be in.

"Now what?" The man who looked back from the dresser mirror had a few more gray hairs than yesterday. Teeth yellowing and his somewhat painful, double chin looked quite a bit more pronounced too. Trevor stared in distress at the height of his forehead, realizing his hairline pulled back further than he'd have liked. "We're getting old fast my friend. Not good."

Since his bedroom was close to the front door, he employed a long remembered trick from his teenage years and managed to sneak out before mom or dad noticed he was awake. Grinning with satisfaction, he depressed the clutch and quietly backed down the driveway before starting the car. Same as it ever was.

At the bottom of the hill, he looked at the strip mall pass by on his left. Lights off and quiet, the Suite Sweet remained the same old trashy dump out of context with everything else in the neighborhood. He sped down Balboa Boulevard spitting on the road he hated all these years.

The old High School was completely different. The buildings weren't the same 1960's institutionalized style they were when he went there. After the earthquake in the early '90s, they rebuilt the entire school from the ground up. Now he didn't recognize anything. None of the initials etched in the walls or band names painted on the bleacher beams were there anymore. All new. A sour burn rose from his stomach to his throat knowing all the good memories were forever stripped away. Whether by the cruelty of nature or by man's greedy hand, nothing could ever stay the same.

The film of his memories flickered in his mind's eye, Trevor dreamt about football games and school dances. The strange and wet warmth when Jennifer Kaplan put his penis in her mouth for the first time. How his chest cracked open revealing his heart to the world when she broke up with him.

He shifted into park and turned off the car before realizing where he was. The Suite Sweet's weathered and swollen door stared through the windshield inviting him in for a drink. There were so many other places he'd rather pass his time than in this dump. He even ran through a list of them while climbing out the door. He pictured the strip club on Sepulveda that had a brunch buffet free with the purchase of two lap dances. Now *that's* the way to spend a hooky day. He could have been relaxing at the Green Door massage parlor in North Hollywood, getting a bit extra for a bit extra. Until the stale fumes slithered into his nose, he didn't realize he already sat at the bar ordering his first drink of the day.

"A man walks into a bar and says..." Artie scooped ice into a rocks glass and set it on the bar. His long frame folded nearly in half, vibrating with silent convulsions. His skin wrinkled while facial muscles contorted themselves into a painful expression that just as easily depicted acute wretchedness as it did elation. Unable to take in enough air to finish the joke, he gripped the inner edge of the bar to keep from falling.

"He says?" Trevor waited impatient for his drink to be filled.

"A man walks into a bar..." The laughing fit attacked again, preventing Artie from pouring the whiskey into Trevor's waiting glass.

"Whew. Okay. I got it now." A long slow pour filled the short glass nearly to the brim.

"Thank you Artie." Trevor took his glass.

"Don't you want to hear the end?" Artie leaned back against the shelves in the spinning shadows cast from the naked bulbs next to his head. "It's one of my best ones."

"I think I'll sit over at the table back there today if you don't mind." Trevor pointed over his shoulder to the empty booth at the wall.

"You will do no such thing kiddo." Bridgit materialized from the darkness at the end of the bar. "We are the day drinkers Caper my boy. This is a rare and time-honored position of importance. When we find another of our kind, we never allow a sip of a drink to pass through their lips while alone." She shouted at the barman with a spry forward thrust of her arm, "Bring us drinks Lurch! Drinks I say!"

"Please don't call me that." Artie crossed his arms across his thin chest staring at the energetic old woman. "I told you a million times."

"Aw go on and grow a pair you big pussy." Bridgit stood, grinning wide. The glint of the swimming lights shone from her teeth. Crisp, white and clean they gleamed like newly scrubbed ivory. Trevor stared for a moment trying to remember what was so different about her face now. "Good morning to you Caper."

"Mornin'." He reached for the glass as soon as Artie put it down on the coaster.

"Ouch." Turning away, the bartender glided down the length of the bar folding his long body onto the bench.

"What?"

"Ouch. A man walks into a bar and says..." Artie paused waiting for the punch line to sink in. "Give it a minute."

"Ouch?" Mid-sip it came to him. Trevor coughed and gagged. He fought against choking, in between spurts of the burning liquid that erupted from his nose and mouth he attempted to speak. "I...get...it." Shaking her head, Bridgit lit a cigarette, humming along with "Muskrat Love" seeping from crackling speakers built into the sides of the jukebox.

Trevor's stomach clenched tightly, a stabbing pain burning from the inside of his belly nearly pulling him down from the barstool. Covered in sweat and groaning, he stumbled to the bathroom knocking into the man in the wrinkled tan suit blocking the path. His fingers dug into the jacket sleeve for balance and pulled the drunken man down to the floor along with him. Battling his body's urgent need to throw up, he shoved the man deeper into the sticky carpet in order to launch himself to the relative safety of tile floors and cool porcelain.

Between the muscle upsurges and wiping his mouth on freshly torn toilet paper, Trevor thought about how to apologize to the man left on the carpet. Buying him a drink didn't seem sufficient. But as he sat in a heap on the floor, cheek leaning against the side of the grime-encrusted toilet, he felt sure something appropriate would come to him.

Trevor caught his breath, waiting to be sure his stomach settled into enough calmness for movement. With no desire to examine the results of his purging, he flushed the toilet without looking and dragged himself out of the stall. The pipes groaned and sputtered out gray, lukewarm water. He let it fill his hands, splashing his face and the back of his neck until a small semblance of clean appeared.

Swishing the water around in his mouth to get rid of the puke taste, his tongue noticed something strange. On the upper right side where his incisor should have been was an empty space. His tongue found its way through, twisting itself sideways to the inside of his lip. There was no blood in the mirror. There was no ache or pain. The tooth simply was not there. He stretched his lips apart with his fingers to look closer. Three molars had disappeared from the lower mouth too.

He screamed, a frightened and wounded child. Staggering back to the toilet , he could find nothing having already flushed. If the teeth did fall in there, they would be long on their way to the Pacific by now. Disregarding that knowledge, he shoved his hand into the drain searching for any remnants of the AWOL choppers. His knuckles, near the extent of fitting in the pipe, popped through the curved porcelain as he pulled them back out of the water. Darting about his mouth, his tongue hoped it would find familiar molar curvature and ease his mounting panic.

Once more at the sink, his head shuddered. His father's face twisted from side to side in strange reflection. Gray streaks edged back from his balding crown to the tops of his ears. The widow's peak he expected to replace with hair plugs in ten more years, now dominated his middle-aged head. Spots mushroomed across the skin of his hands, wrinkles and callused warts swelled before his eyes. Deep cracks and crevasses spread wildly over the map of taste buds on his tongue. His eyes faded from their once brilliant blue into a shadowy memory of the sparkle that could call women across a darkened club into his seldom-idle bedroom.

He limped from the bathroom on tight and resistant legs. Sliding through the shag, his feet fought a losing battle against the carpet's gravity. He fell into the body-shaped depression left by the man in the wrinkled suit, fitting perfectly into its form in the carpet. There was a woman's laughter and a deep voice whispering. The needle scratched over the record again dropping a new platter on the turntable. With no trace of irony Bo Donaldson sang "Billy, Don't Be a Hero."

"So one day me friend Alphie asks me a question." Artie tried on a thick, overtly dramatized cockney accent while he yanked Trevor from the floor in to the heavily stuffed, black vinyl booth. "He says to me, he says, 'Artie?'

So I says, 'Yes Alphie?'

'Artie, wot 'appens to us when we dies?'

'Well, we builds you a big wooden box.'

'What does I need wif a box?'

'We have to puts you in somethin' don't we?'

'You puts me innit?'

'Yes we does.'

'Then wot?'

'Then we digs a deep, deep hole.'

'A hole?' he says. 'Wot d'ya do wif the hole?'

'We drops you innit.'

'Oh. Then wot?'

'Then the bugs come.'

'I don't like bugs Alphie.'

'S'okay Alphie. They canno' 'urt ya. You're already dead.'

'Oh. Right. Then wot 'happens?'

'Then you pops up outta the ground.'

'A zombie?'

'No. You'ain't no zombie. A plant.'

'A plant? Wot kind?'

'A flower, mate.'

'Wot kind of flower?'

'You'd be a daisy.'

'Ooh. I does like daisies I does.'

'Yes you does.'

'Then wot 'appens Artie?'

'Then a big horse walks by and he sees you.'

'I likes horses too.'

'I knows you does Alphie.'

'Does I get to ride the horse?'

'No. Not this one. This horse likes daisies so much, he stops walkin' and he eats you.'

'Oh my. Wot 'appens then Artie?'

'Well, then he drops you on the road.'

'Ew. Then wot?'

'Then I comes by. I comes by and I sees you.'

'That's nice.'

'Yes it is.'

'Then wot?'

'I sees you and I says, 'Ello Alphie you ol' shit, you 'aint changed a bit!'"

"That one never gets old Lurch." The woman's cackle growled across the room, a blanket of jagged glass. Her long hair drifting into the undulating light that spun down from the fixtures above the bar.

"Don't call me that."

"Chill out Stretch Armstrong." She waved a dismissive hand in his direction and blew a deep lungful of white smoke into the already toxic atmosphere's bitter brew.

Glowing with happiness, the young lady took the whiskey from Artie's hand, and shifting daintily across the room, she sat across from

Trevor. "Don't love me." She whispered and pushed the drink to Trevor's hand. He recognized none of the cold glass touching his fingers. He made no attempt to wipe the alcohol from his chin as it drooled from his bottom lip. There was nothing anymore but her.

Strikingly beautiful, he stared at her perfect and wonderful face. Her teeth straight and gentle gleamed between full, not puffy, lips giving him the urge to nibble them. Shoulder length hair the color of honey caressed the rosy slope of her jaw further accentuating the flawlessness of her construction. Her tongue traced the edge of an ice cube. A tiny strand of spittle stretched with it to the bottom of the glass and snapped. His ears tightened at the crack echoing throughout the dark room. The record screeched and stopped. The silence that followed would inhabit centuries.

Her eyes looked back into him opening his private windows wide. She floated into him freely taking books off of shelves, heirlooms from drawers, keepsakes that made up the clutter of his life. His grandfather's silver pocket watch dangled its long chain between her middle and ring fingers. The second hand clicked, though muffled by the silence of time, sliced sharp as a stiletto through his ears. She penetrated deep into his skull to burn away memories, dreams, hopes, happiness.

When she made her exit, she bolted the double doors of his mind behind her. All that remained of Trevor followed her out of him, no longer capable of inhabiting himself. His body collapsed in a lump in the booth holding a half-emptied glass of expensive whiskey, eyes fixated on the woman who sat across the table. A ring of smoke slithered from her lips widening in space until it dissipated into the air becoming another stain on the ceiling.

"Bridgit." Artie wiped down the bar with a crisp, white rag. "Don't take too much at one time."

She shimmied from the booth. "Yes sir." Her hand snapped a mocking salute and pressed her lips delicately to Trevor's ear. The warm breath and moistness of her tongue sent chills through his limp arms. "Thanks for your time Caper."

"I didn't listen... she told me not to ..." The old man sitting in the booth mumbled to himself. "... so beautiful..." The cloud of smoke reached downward, spreading a putrid shroud of exhaled, sullied dreams to never be fulfilled. "...so beautiful..."

Bridgit opened the door into the sunlight. The clicking of her high heels faded away to the other side of the parking lot and beyond. The jukebox found another record and crooned out "Tie a Yellow Ribbon Round the Ole Oak Tree," forever silent to the outside world behind the closed door. Ignored by most people, the sign on the roof continued to flash Suite and then Sweet.

Suite.

Sweet.

Suite.

Sweet.

JOSEPHINE

"You lock the door and put them old records on. I hear you crying along.
Oh what a fool I've been. Oh what a fool I've been.
No more will the final words be the tears in your eyes."

—JASON MOLINA

IT'S HARD TO CLEAN THEM OUT. I pulled out the thin file that's on my fingernail clippers. You know the one. That part we all use to dig the gunk out from under our nails. I think it's supposed to be used on the cuticles or something. But I don't know anyone who uses it that way.

Jamming it underneath the jagged edge of my nail, I realized I needed to get a manicure soon.

I sucked in a quick hiss of air as the point jabbed in too far, probing deep into the tender flesh. Since it's filled with nerve endings that are normally protected from the rest of the world by my dirty nail, it hurt like hell. Lucky for me it didn't go far enough under to draw blood.

I must admit I looked pretty despicable. Three of the lights over the bathroom mirror blew out last week, but I'm just too damn lazy to get around to replacing them. The green counter tiles reflected a swampy hue up toward my chin in the light of the one remaining bulb. I gave myself a Frankenstein grin and returned to the task at hand. Or task at nail for that matter. Cleaning my nails should be much easier, but the file kept getting stuck in the dried gunk.

I heard him in the dining room flipping through my new coffee table book, which featured oversaturated full color pictures of beat up rusted pickup trucks and century-old faded barns that hadn't seen a paintbrush in decades. You'd think it would be boring, but the images held a haunting and familiar quality. Quite spiritual in a way.

"I'll be out in a minute Gregg," I shouted through the oak of the bathroom door. "Sorry it's taking me so long."

"No problem." His voice came from close to the stereo. "I apologize for the inconvenience, but I have to talk with everyone in town. What is this music playing? I like it."

I placed the clippers back on the middle shelf of the medicine cabinet in between a half empty tube of mint toothpaste and the new package of shaving razors I bought last week, then wiped my hands dry on the daisy covered towel next to the sink. "Something my nephew sent me. He keeps me up to date on all the hip new sounds. I love this record." He stood with his side facing me and was holding a disc case and reading the back when I stepped out of the bathroom. I eyed the large revolver resting in the holster on his hip.

Holding up the case he said over his shoulder, "I've never heard of these guys. Nice stuff. I can always rely on you for good music." He put the case back down on top of the stereo and walked over to the fireplace resting his left arm on the mantel.

"I can make you a copy if you like. That is if you won't haul me away in cuffs for breaking the copyright law Sheriff!" I laughed.

He smiled. "I won't tell if you don't." Gregg held his right index finger up to his mouth pretending to shush me.

"Can I get you some water or something?" I walked toward the kitchen and started to root around in the fridge. "I'm all out of coffee and soda. I meant to go to the store this morning."

"No. Thank you." Gregg moved to the window and pulled the blue drapes over so he could look outside, possibly canvassing the area or some other lawman stuff. "Unfortunately this isn't a social visit. I still need to see the Molina's and a few more houses before I head back to the station."

"What do you need Gregg?" I walked back out of the kitchen to the living room having found nothing of interest in the refrigerator.

"I don't know if you heard, but Josephine Field is missing." His hands clenched and I could tell he was upset about it. Gregg was a great Sheriff. He made sure to spend a little time getting to know everyone here in Pastor. We all loved him too. Everybody's favorite uncle. He and I had been friends since we played ball together in high school. I for one wasn't surprised when he went into law enforcement.

Even way back then, he dripped with a commanding air of control in every situation. Whether he was throwing the perfect strike in little league with a three and two count to end the bottom of the ninth, or breaking up a bar fight, Gregg could be counted on to save the day.

"What? Oh my God. Not another one." I leaned on the back of the couch to keep from falling over. This was the fourth time in three years. "What…" Choking hard on the word, "I mean, when?"

"Yesterday morning. She never made it to work at the coffee shop." Eyes closed tight, Gregg raised his head toward the ceiling. "According to Marcia she left for work around 5:30 AM, and no one's seen her since." His voice held steady and matter-of-fact through the entire description. I knew him well enough to hear the tiny shudder when he pronounced his long vowels.

"Marcia who?"

"Marcia Grayden is Josephine's roommate." He explained. "They've been living together for the last year or so." He raised his eyebrows a little. Then he whispered under his breath, "Pretty girls like that ought to have boyfriends if you ask me." I didn't think he meant for that comment to be heard.

Every man in town tried a shot to be with Josephine at some point. Her tip jar was always full with the hopes and fantasies of single and married guys alike. Josephine's genuinely warm personality made everyone around feel good about themselves. She never seemed exactly flirtatious, but not exactly *not* flirtatious either. Those yellow brown eyes of hers could tame any brute.

"What can I do to help?" I asked, grabbing my fur-lined denim jacket hanging on the back of the table chair. "Do you want me to help put together a search party?"

"No." Hands raised, he walked towards me. "Hopefully we'll find her before it comes to that. I just need you to keep an eye out for me again, ok?" He sagged and I could see the weight bullying deep into his shoulders. "We've got to find her."

"Sure Gregg. You will. We will." I reached out and squeezed his shoulder gently. "I'll do anything I can to help. You know that."

Taking the hat off his head he wiped the sweat from the beginnings of a widow's peak with his sleeve. "Thanks man. I know it's a small town, but you're one of the only folks around here I trust to have my back when things go downhill."

I smiled and held my arms open wide. "What are friends for Gregg?" We walked to the door and I opened it for my old friend. The old hinges creaked, singing us on through to the porch.

"Keep your eyes open for strangers and stay by the phone just in case, yeah?" Hat back on his head he could have been Glenn Ford or Gary Cooper in one of those old black and white westerns. He waved over his shoulder, turning toward the cruiser's flashing lights.

Waving at dust clouds kicked up by his tires pulling back on to the main road, I shook my head and locked the door. Couldn't be too careful with the possibility of strangers in town. Closing all the drapes, I turned the volume up. My favorite song on the album took its turn churning the air of my living room. "Oh which one of us is free…Josephine?" I sang along at the top of my lungs.

I slipped the plate of leftovers out of the fridge and pulled off the saran wrap. The sauce was still tangy on my finger when I licked it. Balancing the plate carefully on my left hand I opened the closet with my right. Pushing my musty holiday sweaters and old dust covered letterman's vest aside, I took the metal latch at the edge of the back wall and gave it a twist. The wall pushed back and I switched on the light so I wouldn't trip going down the smooth cement stairs.

It's a small town all right, and I love it here.

THE loneliness
OF LEFT FIELD

"For as children tremble and fear everything in the blind darkness, so we in the light sometimes fear what is no more to be feared than the things children in the dark hold in terror and imagine will come true."

—*LUCRETIUS*

RIP SAW A MOVEMENT IN THE TREES. Yes the wind was blowing and the leaves were swaying, but there was a stirring deep back in the empty black spaces. He scrunched his face to see clearer through the glare because the brim of his Red Sox cap didn't want to do its job protecting him from the sun.

"Heads up out there!" Coach Leatherman shouted. Rip covered his head until the ball thudded the grass a couple of yards away. "Pay attention pal. You should have had that one!"

"Sorry coach." He trotted over to the loose ball and threw it in the direction of second base. The errant throw bounced way off left and Denny stumbled over himself trying to get it. In a scramble of uncoordinated flailing limbs, Tom finally scooped it up, lobbing it back to the frustrated coach.

"We need good throws from you guys in the outfield. Good throws! This is why we've got to back each other up infielders." Coach waved his arms in frustration and continued to shout instructions in ever more explosive tones. Rip's mind was already elsewhere. He didn't like playing left, especially here at Whippett Field. If only coach let him pitch today. The left field fence was much too close to the trees. His house was surrounded by trees that he grew up climbing, swinging from and playing Knights in Shining Armor in. He loved the woods. But not these trees, these trees were just *bad*. There was something wrong with this place.

"Alright Sox!" Coach waved around. "Bring it in!"

Rip jogged back in for the start of the game. When he turned over his shoulder he thought something dark slid between the branches past the fence. He stopped at the infield's edge and strained his eyes to see better.

"Watcha' lookin' at Rip?" Carter stopped next to him on his way in from right field.

"Nothin'." Little clouds of brick dust puffed up behind each foot shuffling their way to the dugout. As the visiting team they surrendered the field to their opponents, the North Camden Astros. Rip usually liked playing in the travel league. Getting to play against kids from different towns and schools was pretty cool. Sometimes the other teams weren't very good and the Pastor Red Sox won easily. These Astros were hitters though. Plus, they looked mean.

"Hey guys, watch the pitcher warm up yeah?" Coach Bill leaned his broad shoulder on the fence in front of the dugout. Bill Darden owned the hardware store in town. Even though he was a year younger, his son Tom and Rip were best friends. It was cool having him as assistant coach this season. He always brought a case of Gatorade in his hand-painted Red Sox cooler for the guys.

Bill walked slowly backwards. Tapping Joe on the shoulder he leaned in close so none of the kids could hear him whisper, "Look at the leaves."

"What?" Joe turned his head making a quick motion as if to brush a buzzing fly away from his face.

"Look at the leaves." He didn't want to point and draw any attention.

"Man, I'm trying to call signs here."

"Joe. Look at the God damned leaves!"

"Okay. Okay Bill. Jesus. Calm the fuck dow…" The toothpick fell from Joe's bottom lip. His eyes couldn't decide if they wanted to squint or stretch open even wider.

There were hundreds of trees. Possibly even thousands sprouting countless numbers of leaves. Leaves that provided shade on hot summer days. Leaves that on any average day breathed in carbon dioxide and exhaled oxygen. Leaves that would eventually fade to the beautiful bright yellows, oranges and reds of fall.

Now every single tree stood stark naked and bare. Empty deep brown branches scratched like sharpened fingernails against the blue sky. The deep green sea of leaves hovered in a thick, motionless straight line four feet above the ground.

One Cardinal hopped its way out from beneath the shadow of leaves up to the left field fence. Its beak reached up and grabbed on to the metal wire pulling itself up. Claws took hold lifting the body higher as it climbed up. Rolling over the top, the bird dropped back down to the ground making no attempt to fly.

A handful of red breasted birds mimicked his ascent over the chain links. Then another emerged from the shadows. Then another. And another. The fence grew loud with the clicking and rattling sounds of birds clamoring over and falling silently to the grass. Hundreds of bright crimson breasts hopped in silence together toward the infield.

Rip stood in ready position. Knees bent, punching his right fist into his glove and anticipating anything hit his way. The first bird hopped a few feet to the left. He saw a hint of red in the corner of his eye. The next bounced down the left field foul line heading toward third base. He tried not to let them distract his focus. Not after coach chewed him out during warm-ups.

He felt something soft brush against his leg. He looked down at the bird walking between his legs. One of its little claws slid across the inside of his cleat. Heart clenched, his young ribcage on the verge of exploding. He jumped away for fear of getting pecked, knocking it to the ground. The bird calmly whipped its wings twice, stood up and continued walking forward, black eyes peering unfocused into the distance.

"Coach?" The flock of birds rolled in a slow tide, each of them striding in unsettling silence. The first scattered few made their procession to Rip's left. More followed close behind out of center field.

Julia threw her best pitch, a curve ball. Darrell Matling took a long drink from the faded plastic of his Big Swig cup, weaving on his feet behind the backstop fence. Half-full with his very own concoction of cherry soda and vodka, the buzz felt pretty good about now. He liked to stand there and watch his daughter pitch knowing she could see his disappointment after every throw. Bat connected with ball. He traced the small white orb dart toward left-center. Instead of sighing in frustration and glaring at the pitiful attempts of his girl fighting to be tough as a boy, his eyes caught an unusual reddish movement in the outfield.

Darrell swiveled his head around and saw that nearly everyone in the stands was looking that way too, with fingers outstretched, speaking in strained whispers. Darrell felt his stomach tighten in a way it hadn't since he heard his own father's belt snap outside the door to his room.

Coach Bill ran on to the field waving and shouting at all of the players. Rip turned around and watched his feet disappear in the swarm of bright red feathers. His arms wheeled in circles knocking the cap from his head. He stumbled backwards tripping over the mindless birds walking ahead. A soft squishing sound accompanied the cracking of bones as the boy landed hard, crushing a handful of them. One bird climbed on top of his legs as he lay trying to catch wind back to his lungs. With no attempt to avoid the boy, it continued walking on his stomach and over the bright lettering printed across his jersey.

"Dad?" He smacked the bird with his glove sending it tumbling across the grass knocking into three others as it rolled over and over. "Dad." Turning onto his front he shoved himself back up to his feet and ran, feet inadvertently kicking small red bodies out of the way. Feathers clung to the smear of moist red glistening on the back of his uniform distorting the number 9 into a nauseating double helix 8. "Daddy!"

Todd McKewan, hearing his son's frightened voice, raised his eyes from the laptop screen in annoyance. "Now what?" Slowly absorbing what they were witnessing, the image of Rip kicking through the red swarm of flightless birds entered in through his eyes and exited through his mouth in a terrified scream. "Rippington!"

The glowing screen tilted and slid from his lap, bounced on the metal footrest and fell with a loud clang. Todd jumped down the bleachers with a speed he wasn't aware he possessed. Not caring about keeping his balance, he tripped over a purse resting on the ground, catching his foot in the shoulder strap. Using the side of the brick dugout for balance, Todd kicked the bag from his ankle feeling the bumps and jabs of other parents' elbows and knees storming past vainly, charging to protect their suddenly fragile young.

Collin Nancarlo edged his black and white past the eleven cars covered with dust in the lot. He stopped next to the unopened snack stand and opened the door. The gravel crunching beneath his boot reached his ears muffled and dampened like the world had submerged itself in Styrofoam.

Still new to the Staties and wanting to beat back the constant hazing and jabs from the older guys, he decided to check things out on his own before calling Rita and the chief at the station. He put the wide brimmed hat on his head relieved to block out the glaring heat of the sun from his face. Turning to face the field, the odd silence disturbed him.

"I thought there was a game this morning." Once again, the sound of his voice became suffocated and brittle in the space between mouth and ear. His eyes scanned the empty field from across the parking lot. "Where is everybody?"

He should have felt a sense of urgency. A rush of adrenaline pumping through veins, muscles and brain. There ought to have been some warning that this was no longer a place of happy family time and daydreams of someday making it to the big leagues. Instead, a soothing calm dripped down his skin relaxing his thoughts and responses. Fingers entwined with the chain links next to the dugout marked Visitors in bold white letters over a background of dark green.

Wind danced in silent circles across the field. Red brick dust on the infield twisted devilishly in one large speckled sheet sliding across the overstuffed white bases. A freshly scraped ball hung in the air on its way to the space between third base and shortstop. A glare of sunlight beamed off the top of a small aluminum bat paused mid-flight, discarded by the hitter just outside of the batter's box.

One chewed up moist sunflower seed shell flipped end over end in the center of a chain linked fence square. Inside the dugout a dark blue helmet was still in its drop from the bench. Spilled purple Gatorade splashed in the shape of a small shoe arcing outward from the center of a small puddle.

Flickering orange ashes from a discarded cigarette butt halted in mid-throw. Pink handles sparkled lifting the jump rope back up from the dirt at the beginning of one more revolution. Ringlets of steam curled thinly upward from hot brown coffee seized in pour over the lip of a white Styrofoam cup. One small Red Sox cap hung inches above the ground in deep left field. The brightly red lettered "B" signaling up to the crystalline blue sky.

Officer Nancarlo opened the gate, slowly walking on the grass next to first base. A high pitched rattling sound pulled his eyes toward the left field fence. Without thinking, his left hand moved closer to the gun holstered on his hip. Cautiously he walked across the infield moving closer to the area where the sound originated.

"Hello?" Air did in fact leave from his lungs into the surroundings. An oppressive thickness made its presence felt more potently by swallowing his words into nothingness before his ears noticed they weren't arriving at their destination. He searched the dark spaces hidden between the trees made all the more impenetrable by the sun bearing down on his eyes. "Where are you guys?"

At this moment he noticed a flicker of motion. Low to the ground a smear of dark red crawled through the shadows emerging at the outfield fence. The young policeman watched as the cardinal bit a bar of wire with its beak, climbing to the fence top with claws grasping and pulling in tandem. Plopping uncoordinatedly to the grass, the bird strolled casually on to the infield, stepping over second base and finally stopping three feet in front of his black leather boot.

"What the…"

The bird faced upward staring directly into his eyes. Perplexed by this odd little visitor Officer Nancarlo looked back into the deepness. The small black ovals showed him there were things about the world he could not understand. A comprehension dispensed by this place that must be avoided. An understanding of things that are not always the way we are brought up to believe.

Collin dropped to his knees. Watching from the road one might have seen a policeman frantically digging away at the infield dirt, screaming silently with his face pressed against the ground. Red feathers catch your eye taking your gaze up to watch a thick bird lift to the sky flying away into the bright. Looking back down, the wide brimmed hat rests flat on the dirt with no head to call home anywhere in sight.

"Collin (static) you there?" The woman's voice is rough from a two-pack-a-day three drink minimum habit. "Hey Collin, (static) Chief wants to know the score of the game (static)." The window of the squad car remains rolled down. "Collin? (static) Hey Col… (static)."

DOWN THE
SUNDAY HOLE

Please allow this, being the first part of a story in progress, to serve as an introduction. While Miss Anne introduces Ro to new perceptions of the world and his place in it, we might find ourselves turning corners, presented face to face with visions and dreams normally reserved for those hours when eyes are closed leaving minds left unguarded...

Come with me Down the Sunday Hole soon.

Ladybug, ladybug, fly away home
Your house is on fire
Your children all roam
Except little Nan
Who sits in her pan
Weaving her laces as fast as she can

1

LADYBUG LADYBUG

ADRIANNA HEATHROW ENJOYED a good chocolate. If her grandchildren brought a box of name brand bite sizes from the candy shop at the mall, she'd grin, give squeezes and pinch cheeks until they turned pinkish sore. The instant their parents backed the safe rectangular minivan down the long, tree covered driveway, those boxes would mysteriously fall directly into the center of the trash can that stood to the left of the three car garage.

Never did she want to appear ungrateful, especially to her family. That was a sin she considered worse than any other. Being ungracious to strangers was one thing, but to family? That would be a completely unacceptable behavior that lay outside her understanding. Besides, she kept a never-ending stash of the good stuff locked up in the back of her sewing room closet.

These particular chocolates weren't bulk manufactured, packaged in shiny paper with eye catching logos that force impulse purchases on the shelves of your local 7-11. Nor would they be recognized by the high and mighty Chocolatiers of France and Belgium, or if you were to look in any fancy pants Patisserie. So good, so tasteful and life altering were her dark and luscious treats, Miss Ann (I'll tell you the story of when she asked me to call her that in a minute.) very rarely shared them with anyone at all.

Miss Ann could never be conceived of as selfish or stingy in the slightest of definitions. If you searched from the first day of human existence until three o'clock tomorrow afternoon, you'd never find a more open and generous soul. So munificent in fact, she gave me much more than I was able to take.

2

MARCH 2013

DONALD AND NANETTE PENDLETON moved to Pastor in the early eighties. Don could have stayed in Boston working for the auto dealership his Uncle Freddie was bound to pass down to him in the next decade. Nan had been offered a terrific teaching job at the prestigious Boston School of Modern Dance. However, unlike most of their friends, they wanted a simpler less stressful life. Looking for nothing more than the green hush of trees, friendly neighbors and enough space for a dog to run around without being tangled up in rush hour traffic in their front yard, they came here.

In a strip mall on the north side of Pleasant Pike, between The Pastor Pizza Paladium and Fish Yargh Us Fresh Seafoods, Nan opened her children's dance school Tippy Toes. Monday through Saturday year round, all the neighborhood daughters could be found spinning in arabesques, working on their pliés and generally twirling a rainbow of dance tights and tutus. Nan performed in every one of the recitals alongside her students, making extraordinary events of them. Full color posters hung all over town and the girls danced door to door handing out personalized invitations in full performance regalia. On the day of each show, the volunteer fire department and state police cars would lead a parade through the center of Pastor blaring music from the Nutcracker Suite over their loudspeakers, followed by rows of Tippy Toes students dancing in the street.

Don't think this was some sort of ego exercise for Nan. Instead of pilfering attention, Nan ducked her way out of the spotlight. Her every move accentuated and complimented the beaming smiles stretched across those little girls' faces, loading the parents' cameras with many of the brightest memories their families would ever know.

Donald settled in to small town life in his own way. His gift from a tour of duty in the Marines, the prosthetic leg he limped on made it difficult to do farm work for any extended period of time. Instead he devoted himself to sculpture. Not schooled in any way other than his love for the physicality of the work, his skill and unique voice developed quickly.

After their first year in Pastor, the Mayor himself requested he create a piece for the Town Hall. To this day the eight-foot tall iron and wood wind-activated mobile called, "Pastor-all", sways gently in front of the capital building's entranceway. Two years later he put on a one man show in Boston's legendary Piperton Gallery. It wasn't much after that his works were being shown in Paris, London, New York and even Hong Kong.

Five years after his Los Angeles debut, their son Thoreau was born. As the bouncing ball of dirt and noise that took center stage in every dance class and art opening, I had a knack for attracting attention. Constantly boisterous and chaotic as possible, my folks encouraged my antics instead of shushing me into a silenced, obedient corner. I wished for a little brother or sister, and I know they did too. Mom almost died when I came around, wrecking their chances to build the brood they dreamed of.

I couldn't ask for better parents. I never met Uncle Freddie or any other family for that matter. They all died before I came along. So, the three of us took on the world. Busy, happy and free. Well, four of us if you count Ace. Attached to my ankle, you couldn't find me anywhere without that black and brown Sheltie causing trouble at my side.

I loved to read. Comic books or paperbacks, our local library was the nearest place to heaven. Dad hoped I'd become a poet or famous playwright. Mom didn't push. She encouraged me to be a seeker, to never stop looking for my passion and follow my instincts. If either of them were upset when I came home from school with a bad grade, they never outwardly expressed it to me. There were many discussions about how "Mathematics is just not your forte." Or, "There are plenty of scientists in the world. We can do without one more right?"

Two months into my sophomore year of high school, the principal called me into the office. Being the free spirited troublemaker I had become, I knew every scuff mark on his floor tiles by then. Since I couldn't be sure which prank summoned me here this time, I dreamed up background stories in my head. Either I'd been called into the girl's locker room for emergency plumbing repair after the toilet exploded, or the M-80 found in Mr. Cornfield's backseat was nothing more than a horrible mystery to me.

Not remotely close to completing the scripts of my speeches, Ms. Balachine lifted the heavy black receiver from her desk. "Mr. Macameaux will see you now Thoreau." She pointed to the smoked glass door with the eraser end of her chewed up pencil. "Go on in."

"Thanks." I hung my head in mock shame preparing myself for the lecture barrage about to volley my way. "Mr. Pendleton. Please, sit." Mr. Macameaux sat in a high-backed leather chair that reached at least one and a half head taller than his natural perm. Tight curls of midnight black hair covered every inch of his small head. Rimless glasses resting in the hair above his forehead forced the only imperfections in the otherwise perfectly rounded sphere.

"How are you today sir?" Attempting unsuccessfully to take the upper hand in our interaction, I wanted to make myself appear relaxed and confident. More likely than not, I came across as smug and childish.

"No need to play kiss-ass... this time anyway." He chuckled once revealing a mouthful of teeth lined with train tracks of thick, dull braces. "Are you familiar with Ms. Heathrow?"

"I think my mom knows her." I recalled some shouting in my general direction for not telling her about a message the old woman left on our answering machine the week before. "Why?"

Only when he walked across to the side of his desk could I tell he was standing. Mr. Macameaux was no more than four feet tall and the chair brought his head to the same height as when he stood. "Ms. Heathrow has recently expressed some interest in your father creating a piece for the school. She is an alumnus of ours you see, and is still very involved in our fundraising."

"Okay. Call my dad then," I reached into my pocket for my cell phone. "Do you need his number?" The tall hair wiggled atop his shaking head. "What does this have to do with me?"

"This morning I had a conversation with your mother." His caterpillar eyebrows crawled higher up the acne scarred forehead. I felt a torrent of panic flood through my bloodstream and squeezed my hands between my thighs to keep them from shaking. What wind-up did they catch me in this time? "She and I both agree that you need something constructive to occupy you out of classroom time. Something to help motivate you toward obtaining more positive goals than say, blowing up the back seat of our history teacher's Honda for instance."

"What?" I screwed up my face feigning a noble attempt at ignorance. "You think that I..."

"Please, Mr. Pendleton." He patted me gently on the shoulder walking behind my chair. "Let's not pretend that I am unfamiliar with your accomplishments. I am well aware of what you are capable and willing to do in order to attract attention to yourself. With parents of such large stature in our community, it is somewhat understandable that you feel a not insubstantial desire to create a name for yourself..." Pulling the string downward, he released light into the room from between the vertical blinds of the large window overlooking the center of campus. "... as an individual. Your parents and I had hoped this need might manifest itself as interest in athletics or the arts. But since nothing seems to inspire you other than disobedience and destructiveness, we are going to attempt placing limitations on your availability to achieve the dominion of mayhem you so desire."

I struggled to come up with a response worthy of the knots constricting my abdominal muscles. Hot sweat beaded my hairline, while cold moistness streaked the back of my neck. My mouth hung open, chin nearly touching my chest. "When... what?" The brilliance of my stiletto-like retort baffled my mind

"After school this afternoon, you will go to Ms. Heathrow's home to discuss your new employment." He handed me a yellow sticky note with an address written on it in blue ink. "She will give you any further pertinent details."

He held up his hand preventing any argument before I could make a sound. "If you hurry Mr. Pendleton, you can make it to class before second bell."

I spent the last half of that day in a quiet daze. Since when did my parents think I was a troublemaker? They encouraged it for Christ's sake. "Always, always be true to yourself", "Follow your muse" and "Don't ever reign yourself in" were the foundations of my personality. I had framed typographic posters of those sayings covering the walls in my bedroom since my first memory of anything. Why did I need a job all of a sudden?

Ace rolled on his back on the center sidewalk outside of campus. Waiting for me same as the day I started third grade. He ducked under a car or one of the buses when it rained. Mom had worked on training him to stay in our yard until I got home, but he chewed through harnesses, ignored electric fences and leapt over wooden ones.

"Too smart for his own damn good." Dad waved his hands giving up on the frustration. "Everybody knows he's Ro's dog anyway. As long as he stays out of the road, what's the harm? Nobody's gonna steal him."

Still hesitant about leaving him, Mom drove by between classes with a water bowl and some treats. She didn't think I knew, but I saw her through my classroom windows from time to time. Next to me, nobody loved that dog near as much.

Walking to Ms. Heathrow's house on Paul Revere Way I called my dad. I hung up instead of leaving a message on his voice mail. Mom picked up on the third ring.

"Hey Thoreau. How's your day?" I heard the usual laughter from young dancers in the background, some of them humming along to Dance of the Sugarplum Fairies. I guessed that was going to be one of her new showstoppers at this semester's event.

"Don't pretend like you don't already know Mom. What the hell?"

"Do me a favor and drop the rebellious teenager bullshit." Apparently some of her students weren't used to her "Mom" tone and quieted down their gaggling. "Sorry girls. Why don't you practice the second section okay? I'll be with you in a tic." A door closed and the music disappeared from behind her voice. "Here's the deal. You are going to see Ms. Heathrow. She is a good friend of mine and your dad's. She is a very proud woman who is getting older and needs more help than she'll ever admit. So squeeze your lemons kiddo. Don't argue. This is how it is." She opened the door letting music and laughter once again fill the background of our conversation. "I love you. Bye."

I stared at the *Call Ended* text on the screen of my phone. The more I thought about it, the more I knew this was the better of the options I could be facing. The unspoken threat of suspension or expulsion seeped between Mr. Macameaux's words. Hell, I could have been arrested for some of the things I did. I never meant to be malicious or spiteful. Causing trouble was simply too much fun to resist.

3

CROSS MY EYES
AND SPIT ON A COMPASS ROSE

THE LONG DIRT DRIVEWAY STRETCHED under cover of thick oak trees obscuring the front of Ms. Heathrow's house. Short stone walls lined both sides curving out of sight and producing a magnetic pull toward the front door. Ace ran ahead, sniffing every inch of the driveway to make sure it was safe for me. Since there was no doorbell, I knocked three times. No one answered. I knocked again thinking I might be able to get out of this if nobody was there to let me in. I slipped my fingers around the doorknob hoping desperately that it was locked. I twisted slightly to the left and stopped before I could feel any resistance.

What is freedom exactly? At that moment it was the sweet release from responsibility. Freedom was the knowledge that the rest of the day was completely mine to waste as I wished. I leapt over the three steps to the driveway and snapped my fingers. "Squeeze my lemons? Okay. Here I go!"

"Mr. Pendleton? Thoreau? I'm guessing that's you." She materialized from behind the right side of the house's wraparound porch, feet making no sound on the loosely stoned pathway. Black hair with scattered white streaks sat tightly wound in a bun on the right side of her head. She wiped her hands on a white cloth and stuffed it into a back pocket of her gardening shorts. "Nan told me you'd be coming by today."

"Hello Ms. Heathrow. Nice to meet you." Dejected, angry and caught mid-escape, I tried my best to hide the disappointment in my voice. Her head leaned to the left, she closed her lips and grinned. Warm and serene, the dark redness in her cheeks radiated a gleaming fire for life rather than the shadowy resolve of death's proximity found as resignation in most peers of her age. Ace barked, bounding past and disappearing around the corner. She watched him go, clicked her tongue against the top of her mouth giving a short, friendly wave inviting me to follow her into the backyard.

The sky hung clear and pure that day with only a few scattered clouds lazily sashaying in their path across the sea of atmosphere. A crimson strip of yarn holding the bun to her head dangled its two ends down near her shoulder. They waved at me as if moving of their own will rather than due to the rise and fall of her short, confident steps.

Rounding the corner, all movement of time snatched out of my grasp. The tree stood near forty feet tall, a writhing tangle of tentacle roots and branches swirled high above the torn ground in a frenzy of gesticulation. Well, the majority of the motion should in fact be explained as finer motor skills, but when I describe what the limbs were doing, you'll understand my meaning. One stem using smaller finger-like branches held a brush to delicately paint white trim around the barn windows. Another tree arm sprayed hose water over the garden full of sprouting vegetation. Two others worked together with a hammer and nail to repair an upended picnic table beneath the shaded porch.

I suppose I shouted. The echo of my voice returned to me from the barn before I felt it leave my throat. Ms. Heathrow turned to me with hair full of long flowing grass, bun now a knot of bark and dirt. Her mouth opened unleashing a shower of muddy seeds, "Thoreau?"

I backed up a step unable to breathe. No more flowers sprouted from the old woman's hair. The barn door's trim remained unfinished and the broken picnic table leaned to one side on the porch. I didn't see Ace anywhere. The enormous oak tree stood silent in the center of the yard. Shade from the long branches embraced Ms. Heathrow like a small, worried child squeezing her mother tightly after too long a time spent apart.

"Thoreau, you look like you just fell down the Sunday hole." The moment she put her hand on my wrist, I felt pure. Not happy or relieved from fear, but pure. Filtering the world through my young, but cynical heart, I'd forgotten what it meant to be alive — how it should be to experience each moment as something new and innocent, slowly tasting every single breath on my tongue and swimming in unexplored waters of discovery.

"What the fuck was that?" I thought out loud.

"I knew you'd be right for the job." Ms. Heathrow giggled and led me to a long porch swing. Gingerly, she wrapped her arm over my shoulders to help me to sit. She crooked her head to the side and winked. "I just knew it. I'll go get you some chocolate milk. Don't you move." Her laughter echoed through the hallway behind the whining screen door. On her way back from the kitchen, she whistled a snippet from the Dance of the Sugarplum Fairies. My feet dangled above the ground, the swing moved gently in the breeze. I felt short as a kid again looking at a world too over-sized for me to reach. Rather than unsettled and terrified, I never wanted to go back to the world before I turned that corner around the yard.

"Drink yourself some of this." She held out a hand painted old mug, worn down from years of use. Shaking from excitement, I took care to hold it in both hands. "Chocolate milk is my all-time favorite. Back when I was little, my daddy always made me a tall glass to lift me up from the dumps. It never failed."

"I feel pretty good now Ms. Heathrow." That first sip — if I existed at all before, I was a mere phantom of the everything I could be and would become if allowed to finish the entire contents of that finger-paint smeared mug in my hands. Everything blurred in front of me, my eyes stretched wide near the point of tearing the corners of my lids apart. I held my breath focusing my ears on the song of a peep toad three miles away serenading his would-be mate. I knew the little girl in Mrs. Johansen's kindergarten class who gave this mug to Ms. Heathrow in 1976. I knew she lived in Santa Monica now with her three young sons and a lawyer husband Jonathan who was cheating on her with his paralegal Craig. I knew the paints were made in a small factory in Beijing by a young child laborer named Umi who missed playing with her pet rat Teddy. The mug itself was made ten years earlier by Liu, the famous half-blind potter of Nanchang.

"Call me Miss Ann. Ms. Heathrow was my momma. I refute that I'll ever be as crotchety or ancient minded as she was." Sitting next to me on the swing, she rolled her bare feet gently back and forth above the stained wood. "Thoreau, I expect you to find that I am neither. I only make those stuffed shirts in the village asking me for money call me Ms. Heathrow."

"Ro," I whispered.

"Pardon?"

"I like Ro." My head swooned. I closed my eyes to catch my bearings, but the brilliant colors of this new world penetrated through my lids enhancing the darkness with fireworks exploding through my mind.

"Then Ro it shall be young man." Her hand slapped my thigh with a strength and firmness I didn't expect from a body that had passed through so many years.

"Ms. Heathrow..."

"Please, Miss Ann."

"Sorry. Miss Ann, not trying to be rude..."

"Oh, by all means do Ro. There is no honesty greater than rudeness kiddo." She cocked her head to the side and grinned again. "Only people I'm not rude to are folks who don't want to hear the truth." She leaned back into the swing pushing us into a greater arc. "And don't you worry about that darlin' little doggy of yours. There is no more splendid a place for him to piss on trees and dig around for rabbits than in the Sunday. But, it appears I've interrupted you. What were you going to say?"

"That's okay." My stomach swooned with the increasing speed of the swing. "You know that I'm only fifteen years old right?"

Instantly her feet stuck to the porch stopping the swing. My stomach lurched expecting the world to keep on swinging. Her eyes squinted and mouth pouted a downward half moon in an exaggerated frown. "You best not be accusing me of filth and foulness Ro."

"No ma'am." My body instinctively leaned away from her on the bench. "I just meant that I'm not allowed to drink alcohol yet is all." I held up the half-drunk mug of chocolate milk as an example.

"Oh Ro, you silly boy." Miss Ann ruffled my hair, patted my leg again and stood. "There is nothing illegal about that milk. Cross my eyes and spit on a compass rose."

"What's in it then?" I stared into the ripples of light brown in my hands.

"It's an old family recipe Ro. Very complex and intricate." She wiggled her fingers witch-like leaning sideways against the railing. "Why, people would pay me mountainous wads of cash for the recipe I'm about to give you for free. You sure you're ready for it?" Already familiar to me, her grin stirred my bellyflies. "Can you be trusted Ro?" Deciding to play along, I nodded. "Now you can't write this down for other folks to find. You've got to keep it locked up inside your head." Gently tapping her temple with the swollen knuckle of her bent index finger, she winked at me again. "You promise?"

"Cross my eyes and spit on a compass rose." I winked back.

Miss Ann twirled around twice pointing her toe out at the stop. Every inch of her body projected delight. "The right man for the job indeed." Bouncing up and down without ever taking her feet from the ground. Her hands stretched out coming to rest on my shoulders. Once again I felt at ease and my mind begin to open in a way I didn't know how to prepare for. Her lips pressed into my hair on the crown of my head and she whispered, "Milk and chocolate."

"Milk and chocolate." My lips formed words, lungs pushed air through my throat. No sound climbed through my voice box, only a whispered silent repetition of understanding that Miss Ann had many more simple recipes leading to secrets from the world I might be about to learn.

"Are you ready to get to work?" She held the screen door open waving me into the embrace of the big old house.

4

IN THE HOLLOW

MY LEGS SENT NO FEELING OF MUSCLE MOVEMENT to the brain, gliding across the oddly shifting floor behind the old woman. The house further informed me of its age by its unleveled surfaces and low ceilings. A chorus of creaks and groans harmonized with the breeze flowing in through the open windows. Boringly pale-framed photographs hung near the ceiling on almost every wall. Each one I passed seemed older than the last with the blacks and whites retreating further and further into the paper and losing hold of their developed images.

I didn't see it until Miss Ann turned left at the bottom of the staircase. Every photograph had one similar trait connecting them. The bottom third of each portrait depicted great, bulbous roots of an enormous tree clawing their way out of the dirt. Each cracked pattern of bark mapped slightly different crevasses, though all remained part of the same tree. On top of the largest root, each person captured in the images stood outfitted in fine Sunday filigree. If he were male, his shoes gleamed brightly in the sun with crisply ironed slacks hemmed clean, resting precisely in the same spot. The women wore the exact same hand-stitched blossom-covered dress stopping directly between ankle and knee above bare feet with plain, undecorated toe nails.

Centered in the images, the tree grew wider with the same patterned splinters and knots ending just as the first branches reached away from the trunk. The same furniture rested in the same positions spread wide across the landscape. To the left of the tree, a paint-chipped watering can sat on a round white table. A small bouquet of four freshly picked roses lay beside it tied together with a darkly shaded ribbon. A tire swing hung down from one long rope on the right side of the tree. Shabby and torn, a stuffed animal hung draped through the center of the rubber wheel, and was the sole item in the pictures not in focus, its head and four limbs covered in thick, dirty fur making it more difficult to distinguish exactly what kind of animal it was supposed to be.

The top third of the pictures struck me the most odd. Each subject portrayed in the shots, male or female, ended at the base of their neck. The photographer cut off every single head leaving the shoulders an empty shelf. These portraits were otherwise perfect in every detail, clearly displaying individual stitches of clothing and specks of dirt on the ground, while the veins in the flower leaves and lumps of the different shaped clouds drifted across the background sky. The only thing missing were the people's heads. Once the image reached the torso's peak, the photos ended, abruptly cut off by the thin wooden frames lined up evenly with the ceiling. Curious if the bodies continued on the second story, I placed my foot on the first step to climb.

"Ro, I want to show you something," Miss Ann called from around the corner. I looked into the dark space above the stairs, tentatively changing direction to follow her voice into the parlor. The upright piano faced a wide bay of three large windows. Flowing brown drapes rippled gently with the breeze and covered our view of the outside. She stood next to the instrument resting a hand on the closed lid. "Do you see this?" A life-sized painting of an eighteenth century gentleman hung over the most enormous fireplace I'd ever seen. The hearth stretched from one end of the room to the other, piled with enough chopped wood to keep the entire valley warm for a week. "This is my Great-teenth Grandfather Andrew. He owned everything from the Atlantic to here."

"Did you say Great-teenth?"

"It's easier than saying 'great' thirteen or fourteen times. I lose count." Looking at his face, they shared the same small nose and proud chin. If the colors in the painting were correct, the yellow-green glow in her eyes had been handed down the family line as well. "He preached his church beneath the tree in our yard before the village built up that ugly monstrosity they use nowadays. Pastor Andrew Heathrow. He's why they named this place Pastor. Did you know that?" I shook my head. "Do you ever go to church Ro?"

"No." I felt the bumps on my arms grow cold with nerves at the question. "My parents aren't religious, so they never made me go."

"And how do you feel about that?" She held her eyes away from me on the painting.

"I guess I never really think about it."

"Do you believe in God?" I shrugged my shoulders.

"I shouldn't intrude on your privates. We've only just met." Her cheeks flushed a deep shade that filled in the spaces between her freckles. "It's okay. You don't have to tell me if you don't want to." She motioned for me to sit on the couch across from where she stood. "We'll find out over time anyhow. I assume your mother told you why you're here?"

"I'm supposed to do some work for you."

"It seems you're quite the troublemaker down at my old school. Or am I mistaken?" Once more she angled her head and winked at me. I couldn't help but smile letting her know she had me pegged. "Good for you." Her hands smacked loudly against her thighs. "If you're not causing trouble at your age, what's the point? I'm still making a fuss much as I can these days. No more fun way of living if you ask me."

"Mr. Macameaux said something about my dad too."

"Yes. Your father is an incredible artist." Her eyes stretched wide with a powerful glare of astonishment.

"So everybody tells me." Growing up in Pastor, the immense talents of both my parents were inescapable. I tried not to let it upset me too much, because I knew it was true.

"Well, this is where our work arrangement enters into the frame." Scratching a long wooden match, a thin blue flame reached up into the air from its tip. Slowly making way from one end of the fireplace to the other, she lit kindling beneath the stacked wood, the chimney swallowing the smoke without so much as a fume spreading throughout the otherwise clean and fresh air smell of Miss Ann's house. "I need you to be my assistant. Think you can help me out Ro?"

"What do you need an assistant for?" I watched the hot paper and twigs simmer quickly, blossoming red-orange flames licked the crackling and popping larger logs. Tremendous heat spread through the room, I pulled at my collar and rolled up my sleeves.

"I asked your daddy to create a piece for me using only materials that I provide." She stared beyond the fire into the spaces behind. "Having no artistic talents myself, it's the only way I can really give anything of true value back to Pastor, other than donating my family's money of course." I watched her face lose its smile, nose turning red from the hot air directly in front of her. "When the fire dies down..." Her voice trailed off into an empty silence sucking every drop of energy from the enormous room.

"When the fire dies down?" I leaned forward in my seat.

"I'm sorry Ro." She laughed. "I got lost in my mind there. I've placed a few things in the fireplace that I'd like him to start with. After supper they should be ready to go. Do you like music?"

"Yeah"

"To the stereo boy!" Miss Ann pranced across the room to a waist-high mahogany cabinet. She carefully raised the top section revealing a turntable with a black plastic arm that bent at ninety degrees hovering above a black platter. Behind the doors on the front of the box were two shelves lined with neatly organized rows of album sleeves. Unlike most of my classmates, I knew what they were. Dad still played selections from his giant vinyl collection whenever he was out working in his studio.

My ears jerked backward involuntarily, hearing the needle scrape in between the grooves. She gently set the album cover down against the turntable. The artwork faced away from me so I couldn't see what she'd put on. Her hands open, she caressed the sounds flowing in the air from the speakers, conducting along with the familiar recording. A choir of women's voices plaintively intertwined wordless melodies drawing tears from Miss Ann's closed eyes. Her mouth formed the vowel shapes intoned by the singers. Though not recognizable as any language I knew, my bones comprehended every word.

Flames in the hearth swayed side to side, hovering a foot above the chopped logs. A hollow formed in the center of the blaze providing a clear glimpse of the brick wall on the other side. The choir of voices climbed to higher octaves. Blackened bricks dissolved, leaving in their place a rolling hillside of shimmering jade grass. Standing out against the shocking cobalt sky stood one solitary tree hosting leaves of myriad colors. Large branches became arms. Smaller branches turned to hands with writhing fingers spread wide. Swirl printed leaves curled, conducting the weeping melancholy choir.

Thin coils of gold wrapped around the tree, subtly pulsing in an arrhythmic heartbeat defining a line between the world of the tree and my side of the flames. The music dissolved in slow decrescendo, fire diminishing along in time. In the resulting terrible silence, my ears pained for more. I ached to step through the hollow in the flames. To be held in the brilliant arms of the tree. To be faultless in that unspoiled place. To be perfect.

When I woke, shadows reached long across the room. Through the window, golden remains of sunset faded into a dark blue, above it a deep purple and finally black pierced with specks of far away stars. Miss Ann sat on the couch opposite me staring into the ashes piled in short mounds scattered throughout the fireplace. I rubbed my eyes seeing flashes of the color tree behind the heels of my palms. Yawning, my head quivered taking the images of my dream away to the recesses of my mind.

"How was your sleep?" Miss Ann spoke softly, sounding more than a little sad.

"I'm sorry. I didn't mean to—" She waved away my apology.

"The music takes you where you need to go." Her lips hardly moved. "Ro, I'm glad you're here. We've got so much to talk about you and I. Tomorrow you're going to help me pick out some more pieces for the sculpture. Most of the items I'd like to use are too heavy for these old arms to lift. That's one of the reasons I need a young man like you. But, I'm guessing you have a pretty sharp eye of your own. Maybe even two of them." She winked. "After all, you saw the trees."

"How could you..." I swallowed hard. "That was in my head. How do you know what's in my head?"

"I don't." Miss Ann rubbed her hands on her knees. "The fire showed you the color tree." She didn't pause for my reaction. "My helper tree was in the yard when you got here. I saw you seeing it. Don't worry, you ain't not crazy." She looked back into the fireplace sighing. "Don't forget to remember to breathe now."

My chest burning, I gulped air. The room sucked in around me, walls bowed in a gesture of respect. I breathed out and everything righted itself returning to its original dimensions once again.

"Don't ask any questions tonight. I'm tired and you need to bring the first batch to your daddy for me." She picked up a long poker shuffling through the gray ashes. "Do you see that?" She pointed past the edge of the fire line to what looked like a crispy black baby's hand. "There should be six of them in here. While you dig them out, I'll get the carriage you can use."

Without looking at me again, Miss Ann walked through the long shadows out of the room. Cemented into my seat, I willed my legs to stand and get me out of there. Instead, I wobbled to my feet and moved closer to the fireplace. "No." Hearing my voice out loud I was able to stop. Nothing made sense. Panic ran down my face in droplets of cold sweat. I turned wanting to run for the door.

One bright orange leaf rested in the exact spot where I'd been sitting. It glowed brightly in the shadows, reflecting a light that wasn't there. I closed my eyes not wanting to be fooled by them anymore. She put something in my drink. That had to be it. This was all some kind of hallucination or I was still asleep.

I slapped my cheek hard enough to pool blood under my skin. I didn't wake up. I bit down on the inside of my lip. I didn't wake up. Too terrified to look again, I balled my hand into a fist and slammed it into my groin. I didn't wake up. Instead my body doubled over, collapsing to the floor in a pathetic heap.

"What are you doing Ro?" Small wheels wiggled and creaked under the wooden carriage. "You're still awake if that's what you're wondering." Kneeling down, she placed her hand on my head. "Please stop hurting yourself. You don't have to be afraid right now."

"I don't understand."

Gently, she took my hand guiding me to my feet. "You're different. Like me. Most people never see them. The trees only give a few of us the chance to experience their part of the world."

"Their part of the world?"

"Ro, everything is so much more than you've been taught to believe." Reaching into the fireplace, she wrapped her fingers around a burnt arm and laid it gently in the carriage. "Now, help me bring these arms to your daddy. You'll see more in time. I can't promise you'll understand it, but the trees seem to like you. They might show you more than even I can see. Wouldn't that be exciting?"

"Not really." I wiped my running nose on my shirt. "No." Before she could say anything, I tumbled through the house, past the headless pictures, out the front door and down the driveway. Imagining long, sharp splintered fingers scratching at the back of my shirt until I reached the street, out of breath dripping in sweat despite the coolness of the evening breeze.

I didn't look back. I couldn't. Her voice called my name. My feet flew one after the other not providing an opportunity to listen. I didn't want to. Pictures spun in my head of Miss Ann standing in the doorway, bun of hair/dirt tightly pinned to the side of her head, the giant tree's branches twisting slowly around the house, their leafy fingers intertwining with the old woman's hands. Thicker limbs coiled together beneath her into a bench that hung from vines where she would sit. Swinging calmly, her feet swaying playfully in the air above the porch, her head leaned in the opposite direction of the hair bun. Through the winkles and hints of liver spots, an impish, mischievous little troublemaker appeared with a wink. That's what I pictured anyway. After that afternoon I wasn't sure of anything

5

YOU CAN'T JIGGETY JIG

ONE THING ABOUT LIVING THIS FAR AWAY from Providence is the tremendous number of trees. Endless columns of them line either side of every street. They shade every yard. Many houses have branches leaning far enough over their roofs to intercept smoke escaping from the chimneys. Younger sprouts stretched high to caress lower windows, aching to someday protect the people inside from oppressive summer heat and bone shattering winter chill.

Every wind creak a whimper, leaves falling tears. Trees reached for me from the widest points in my peripheral vision. They waved and curled their leaves for me to go back. Longer branches unfolded themselves across streets and over cars to grab hold and capture their prey. My back muscles flexed, pulling me forward beyond their splintery reach.

Working on a 1957 Chevrolet in his garage, Mr. Sylvain curiously watched me screaming down the street. He didn't see the shadows shift. He didn't notice the thirty foot tall oak in his side yard lean over the fence spreading its long arms toward me. He didn't inch away in fear or retreat inside the house and lock the doors. Instead, he waved a wrench at me and turned his head back to the troublesome, malfunctioning carburetor.

Michael Rosenberg threw the football deep a split second before Matt Cho counted five Mississippi and jumped past the invisible line of scrimmage between the rusted Ford Taurus and the lamp post. Invisible to them, the branches spread the tiniest bit wider letting the long Hail Mary arrive in Willy Mallory's freckled hands for a touchdown. Instead of running home screaming for their lives in terror, they stood in the middle of the street stomping their sneakers arguing if Matt sacked Mike before he threw the ball or not.

Rick Berger climbed the ladder of the Pastor Volunteer Fire Department Engine No. 1 with callused, confident hands. Little Becky Snow's cat, Barley, refused to come down from the old Sugar Maple in front of the post office on Pastor Pike. The fat orange tabby strolled out to the middle of the tremendous branch crossing high above to the other side of the street. Rick would have let it be except Becky's older sister Lindsey's body was a burner. It couldn't hurt his game to score some points with the kid. Plus, the Pike was full of traffic most of the time and his conscience would probably creep up on him if Becky got hit by a car trying to get the damn cat by screaming at it from the middle of the road.

"Barley," Becky pleaded to the indifferent feline safely from the sidewalk. "Please come down. Please"

"I got him Becky." Rick smiled down to the frightened girl. "Don't worry." In the brief moment his attention turned away, the sugar maple twisted ever so slightly bringing Barley close enough for Rick to reach without falling off the ladder. His head so full with fantasies depicting the color and transparency of Lindsey's underwear, this minute change in location never registered.

Though my mind dreamed of re-entering the safety of familiar territory, my heart understood that condition was no longer reachable. Standing outside the door of my dad's studio, I felt every tree watching me. A soft wind carried the scent of burning fireplaces through the yard. Branches swayed and leaves fluttered knowing full well that I could see them now.

"Que paso muchacho?" Dad peeked up from his drawings as I closed the door. "Hey, shouldn't you be at Ms. Heathrow's place? Some kind of work release situation?" His electric eraser buzzed against the paper, forever removing mistakes from any possible view.

"I'd rather be expelled." I stood next to him shaking. "I think she drugged me Dad. She put something in my drink."

"Here we go." Dad's knuckles whitened, tightening his grip on the machine.

"I saw things. Weird things. I mean, whatever she gave me is fucking with my head." The more I said the words out loud, the more I knew how bad it sounded.

"You saw things." He threw the pencil down on top of his drafting table, shaking his head. If cartoons were to be taken seriously, smoke streams would have shot from his ears accompanied by a screaming whistle. "Like what?"

"The trees... waved at me." I looked down at the mud splattered on my sneakers.

"Okay." He took a deep breath and his mouth counted to ten silently. I watched his lips shudder, though I'm sure he didn't know they were doing it. "Have you ever heard of this thing called wind Ro?"

"It's not the wind Dad. The trees are after me." The more I opened it, the more craziness escaped from my mouth hole.

"Calm down Ro. I'm pretty sure Ms. Heathrow wouldn't drug you and the trees aren't *after* you." His forced smile did little to hide the frustration boiling his blood. Dad was never a good poker player.

"Why would I make this up?" It sounded like a perfectly reasonable question to me at the time.

"Because, you don't want to be held accountable and accept your punishment." Dad leaned back in his chair, lifting the front two legs off the floor.

"Come on Dad."

"No." The chair thumped back to the ground. "You come on. I've never had an issue with you expressing yourself. I've always supported you being creative. But when you start damaging other people's property and more importantly put them at risk for harm, we've got a serious problem Roledo." His voice grew louder as the anger overcame his normally mellow and controlled demeanor.

"Dad..." He was no longer in a mood to let me make excuses.

"I've been commissioned to do this piece. It's very, very important. You are going to help Ms. Heathrow in whatever way she needs to make it happen." The electric sharpener buzzed around the broken tip of his pencil. He blew on it making sure there were no traces of dust left to interfere with his lines. "So I expect you to pick up the phone, call her and apologize." Adjusting his prosthetic leg, he shifted on the chair.

"You don't understand Dad." I pleaded with him one more time "I'm not safe there."

"I do understand. I understand all too clearly Ro. End of discussion."

"You're not listening Dad!" I thought if I described some of the things I'd seen, he would understand that I was telling the truth. "The pictures are all fucked up... the fireplace... trees...and Ace is gone!"

"No. You're not listening to *me*." I jumped. He turned into a rabid dog barking at the mailman. "This is the way it is. You're lucky you didn't end up in juvie. The favors and strings we had to pull... This is it Ro. Don't even bother mom with this pal. We're together one hundred percent. You are working for Ms. Heathrow every day after school no fail, no excuses and no more bullshit! Do you understand?"

There was no point in taking this any further. He'd never been this angry with me before.

"Don't give me any attitude on this. You weren't careful enough in the slip." He brushed the hair back from his face and adjusted his thick, round-rimmed glasses. "You drove too fast on the ice pal. Slipped and crashed. You fucked up and got caught. It's time to pay the price." His voice lowered in register back to the more familiar sounds of my Dad. The fight was over. He won. The end. "Do you have any homework?"

"Yeah. Some English and a few pages of Algebra." The heat on my cheeks pulsed along with the blood surging from my uneasy heart.

"Get it done before dinner." Returning to his work, the pencil scraped against paper leaving beautiful lead etchings two dimensionally portraying what would soon stand in the world as a fully developed masterpiece.

"Yeah." I turned my back and opened the door, watching the branches carefully from the safety of the studio before I walked out.

"Hey," I heard him before the door closed. "I love you Ro."

"Yeah." My head on a swivel side to side, I made my way cautiously across the ten yards between the studio and kitchen door, my body curving inward, attempting to escape the imaginary fingers clawing at my skin.

Loud music bounded through the house. The Sugarplum Fairies were taking up residence along with us for the next few months until the recital was over and Mom picked the next piece to awe the neighborhood parents and carpet crawlers. Mom flourished across the open doorway to the living room, a long blue ribbon trailing behind her. I took off my shoes and with socked feet silently brushing over the floor, tried to climb the stairs without attracting her attention. A confrontation with another parental unit would not lighten my mood. Besides, fighting a battle I knew I couldn't win was definitely not my idea of a good time.

"Hey Thoreau." The Fairies were apparently on Mom's side. She stood at the bottom of the stairs looking up at me breathing hard. "How is Ms. Heathrow?"

"Really fucking scary," I emphasized my words so she would know without a doubt that no sarcasm was intended.

"She called a few minutes ago." Mom laughed and using a sleeve, wiped the sweat from her forehead.

"Did she say anything about Ace?" She shook her head questioningly. "She did say you took off like a rabbit though."

"Yeah, guess I did." I grasped the handle of my bedroom door coating it with a layer of hand sweat. "Look Mom, I already had it out with Dad. Can you give me a break please? Got shit loads of homework to do."

"Language. Come down here please." She sat down at the dining room table. "I'm not going to ask again." I dropped my backpack on the floor and moped down the stairs. She stared at her pyramid folded hands until I stood across from her. "Sit down Thoreau."

"Fine. Here's the part where you tell me how I need to take this seriously. You and Dad saved my ass and no matter what I say you're not going to believe me." Obviously I let the sarcasm get the upper handhold on my mood.

"Shut up." That shocked me. She'd never said those two words to me before. "I have to tell you something and you need to hear me. *Really* hear me." Her lips fiercely tightened in a thin line across the bottom of her face. "Ms. Heathrow is important to Pastor. She's more important than your Dad or me. And yes, she's more important than you. Maybe I've been too easy on you. Letting you get away with too much and not... spare the rod and all that crap."

"I'm sorry Mom." I don't know where they came from, but the tears exploded from my eyes running down to my hands folded together on the table. "But I can't go back there. The trees..."

"Yes. You can. Yes. You will." Her flattened palms smacked the polished wood, stabbing my ears. "I don't want to hear any whining about it. Thoreau, she is paying your father an extremely important honor asking him to make this piece for the village. She needs your help, and so does he.

We're bending over backwards to help you out here Thoreau. I don't think you realize how much trouble you got yourself into. She personally stepped in and is making sure the police give you another break. It's either you play along, squeeze your lemons and help Ms. Heathrow out or..."

"Or I go to jail." Why did I have to put the damn M80 in Mr. Billard's car?

"Do not pass go. Do not collect a hundred bucks." She held her head in the palm of her right hand. "I won't apologize for this kiddo. It's not my fault. Things are going to be really different around here from now on."

"Like the saying goes," my lungs jerked the words out, almost coughing. "I guess I can never go home again." My chair screeched on the wood. I stomped up the stairs.

"And you never will." She didn't mean for me to hear it. I grabbed my backpack and watched her bury her face in her hands. Her back shuddered, the muffled sounds of crying followed me into my room.

6

THE NERVOUS MACHISMO
of GENDER GAMES

or

WHERE'S MY DOG, LADY?

TOO DISTRACTED TO FOCUS ON THE PAGES of "Animal Farm" or find the value of X, I opened my laptop and asked Google about Adrianna Heathrow. 28,500,000 hits appeared for "Adrianna" and 31,700,000 for "Heathrow", but nothing with them together. "Andrew Heathrow" didn't bring up anything either. I figured he would at least be mentioned on some Pastor History buff's page. If the Heathrow's were so important to the village, why wasn't there any information about them anywhere?

Dinner was uncomfortable. Forks clinking and knives scraping against the surface of plates ventured the only forays into the deep thicket of quiet. Mom grinned at me a couple of times between bites. Dad only looked up from his food to find his wine glass or reach for another helping of brown rice. I didn't eat much. I couldn't remember the last time Ace wasn't sitting under my chair waiting to snatch falling bites. My stomach churned every time the wind blew through the branches outside the dining room window.

"Do you guys know anything about Andrew Heathrow?" The question blurted out of my mouth much louder than I intended. Mom choked on her chicken, coughing into her napkin.

"What?" she scraped out.

"Andrew Heathrow." I watched Dad pat Mom on the back. "Miss Ann told me that he was the guy who founded Pastor. He's her great, great, great, great grandfather or something." They looked at each other quietly for a beat.

"I think there's a portrait of him hanging inside town hall." Dad stood to get another bottle from the wine fridge. "I remember that name from someplace."

"There's no information about him online. Not even on the Pastor Historical Society page." Talking to them helped to calm the jitters that came every time a gust flushed scratching noises through the leaves. Surprising how my parents could still do that for me.

"I've heard some stories." Mom took a sip from Dad's glass and handed it back to him. He stared at her, eyes turning to slits. "Some of the moms like to gossip and smoke when we take breaks during my classes."

"Like what?" Chicken juices slipped down my throat.

"Nothing that'd hold any water I'm sure." She backpedaled. "Did you finish your homework?"

I nodded, lying. "What did they say about him?"

"Who?" she scooped another serving of rice on to her plate and added to the small mountain Dad barely touched.

"What did the moms say about Andrew Heathrow?" She dabbed the napkin over her bottom lip and then wiped it across the back of her neck.

"Well, I'm stuffed." Dad pushed his plate away. "That was delicious, babe." He placed his dish on the floor and whistled sharply. "Ace. Food."

"Thanks Donnie." Mom spooned up her last few bites. Dad limped across the room, with Mom tailing closely behind. "Can you clean up the dishes Ro?" The sliding door swished open and closed. "Thanks kiddo." I sat alone, a martini shaken and stirred. Their avoidance of Andrew Heathrow added to the fraying of my nerves already raw from my visit with Miss Ann.

"That was weird." The dishwasher sloshing in the kitchen, I dried my hands on a towel hanging over the edge of the sink and looked at the creamy light glowing through the window of Dad's studio. I wondered what they were talking about in there. To me, their conversation could only be circling around two different subjects: One, my continued disruptive tendencies and what bamboo slivered form of punishment they would need to hammer under my fingernails. Or two, the mysteries of Andrew Heathrow and how to continue avoiding the subject until I forgot about him altogether. Personally, I preferred the former. More likely, it was the latter.

I sat in front of the brown upright piano across the room from the fireplace. I never took the time to learn to play. I felt warm drops fall on my fingers. I wiped the moistened keys ringing out a few random notes. Melancholy blossomed deep within my chest, a garden of dejection songs. I thought about all of the things I never learned to do, that I never found the courage to do. No first kiss. Who would want to go to the homecoming dance with me anyway? All the romance movies I used to watch sitting on the couch with Mom. I studied the leading man dialog and tried to summon enough testicular fortitude to talk to a pretty girl. My mouth labored at passing grunts and mumbles, while my mind screamed every smooth and confident line I wanted so badly to say.

Dad's plate remained full in the same spot on the floor where he left it. "Ace?" That dog never let a crumb sit for more than ten seconds, let alone a full plate for this long. I inhaled and puckered my lips ready to blow a sharp call, but my lungs held steady. What if he didn't follow me home from Miss Ann's house? I had to go back and find him.

Outside the winds blew branches in their steady miserere against the roof. Shadows turned to fingers calling for me to come outside. I opened the sliding glass door, feeling a strange tenderness to the icy air. My skin prickled, the pads of my feet tickled over blades of grass crossing the lawn to my Dad's studio. I listened at the door, knuckles pressed gently against the unpainted wood too apprehensive to knock.

"Hey guys?" I spoke through the closed door to the silence on the other side. "Don't make me go back. I can't go back there." Branches scraped against each other as the only reply. "Can you just call to see if Ace is still there? Please?" The guilty feelings about my lost dog were not strong enough to push through my fears of going back there at night. "Please?"

I waited for a long time. No answer. Leaves slid over the ground stopping inches before climbing over my feet. Orange, yellow and red piles grew large enough for me to jump in and roll around like I used to in the autumns of what seemed forever ago. I left them behind and walked back to the house. Keeping the window open over my bed that night, a faint hint of smoke washed into my nose bringing dreams of a luminescent auburn fire with grinning teeth gnashing ragged empty spaces out of the world.

Sleep evaded me like a criminal on the run that night. Adrenaline surged through my muscles near the point of pain. Pacing in circles around the room, I kicked at the dropped socks and discarded sports equipment littering the floor. Eventually an oval shaped pattern emerged tracing my path from the side of the bed to the door and back.

The wind blew hard and every scratching noise across the side of the house caused me to cringe. My mouth begged for moisture having dried into Sahara gulps with no sign of an oasis for miles and miles. Finally giving in to exhaustion, my legs sat me on the edge of the bed as I anticipated the peaceful oblivion of sleep.

Eyes closed, still sitting upright the window crashed inward. With terrible swiftness the branch shot around me from behind and lifted me into the air. Before I managed to struggle, it pulled me through the jagged bits of glass making certain not to cut me. The wind howled past my ears. It's quite possible however that the noises I heard were my screams.

Bending from the thick trunk, the tree passed me to another towering over our neighbor's house. From there the trees continued ushering me from limb to limb until gently placing me down at the foot of Miss Anne's meandering driveway.

7

FEELING WELCOME

I EXPECTED TO SEE FLAILING LIMBS painting and shoveling or performing intricate carvings on the sides of a freshly kilned pottery vase. Every mild puff of breeze sent me ducking against the side of the house or falling to the ground for cover. When the giant branch stretching across the yard creaked, I blurred over the four steps to the porch and stood shivering behind the bench swing. I pleaded it was enough to stand guard between me and the horrible, leafy monster dangling in the wind of Miss Ann's garden.

"What're you doing Ro?" She laugh-barked through the screen door. Bare feet briskly slapping the wooden floor, cheeks shimmering ripe apple red. "You should see yourself. And that screech that come outta you? I thought there was a dying cat in the yard." She waved me inside the open door. "Glad to see you came back."

"You didn't give me much choice." Following her into the front room, I noticed the house was thinner than the day before — ceilings higher and walls cleaner.

"Well, you're welcome here all the same." She sat on the piano bench facing the center of the room, mouth and eyes closed. In the moonlight surrounding her from the tall window behind, she glowed with the peaceful serenity of the dead. "I guess your parents finally told you why I need your help."

"I'm supposed to help you and my Dad with his new sculpture." The fireplace looked much smaller than yesterday. "They didn't give me any details."

"No. They wouldn't would they?" When she stood her finger brushed over a couple keys on the simple instrument behind her back, echoing its discord through the large room. "They didn't tell you because I didn't tell them. But you already know why I need you. Don't you Ro?"

Sweat drained down the backs of unsteady calves soaking through my socks. Muscles trembling and suddenly ice cold, my arms fell limp. I watched the now "normal sized" fireplace follow Miss Ann's path across the room's length. Ash and brick slid in silence from one end of the wall to the other, leaving behind a dark trail that blended slowly into the old, yellowing paint.

"Don't worry Ro." Her hands patted my shoulders from behind. "Nothing here will ever hurt you." Her breath tickled my ear. Words became the wind outside. Wind became leaves rushing across the ground and branches scraping the rooftop. "You belong here."

She sat herself cross-legged on the floor by the wall. Toes wriggling, slightly brown and dirty, shoes obviously not being a common addition to her wardrobe. The hearth dragged sideways across the wall once more, outlining the shape of her proud shoulders in flameless, dark chocolate embers drifting into the air. "Don't you feel the welcome?"

Deep within its center, the violent throbbing in my arms and tightening muscles throughout the rest of my body stretched out with an unfamiliar but serenely warm flush of lightness. I spread my fingers wide in front of my face. Freckles grew and blended with one another covering every wrinkle and scab. Bending my knuckles created a crackle not unlike a campground fire pit. Now completely closed by a thick overgrowth, the inability to open my mouth muffled my voice. Miss Ann rocked while humming a gentle melody to herself. The notes resonated so deeply, the floor shook beneath us rattling every piece of furniture from its allocated place.

"Ro?" her voice circled around the inside of my head. "Do you know why you're needed?" Unable to speak, I shook my head. "If your father and I are going to create a bridge, you need to be the branch between." A sharp sting of soured citrus floated through the room causing my eyes to well. The tears were immediately absorbed into my newly rough, hardened skin. "The Unfading have been watching you. They knew when your seed appeared..." she eagerly held her breath "...the greatest possibility in generations..." Her words evaporated along with her body into the cloud of rising ash in the hearth. Moist sticks remained on the floor in the shape of crossed legs and curling toes.

Leaves scrambled in through the tall open windows. Dust followed by clumps of black dirt coated the walls and ceiling, leaving the floors clean and bright. A brittle and cracked hand gripped the back of my neck. With new parent carefulness, it lifted me from the floor to hang exposed in the center of the room. Long and thin, pale arms reached for me through open and scatter cracked windows. Cautiously, fingers with leaves for nails brushed themselves along my skin. At each touch, my body pulled away until their gentleness reassured the fight or flight instinct that there was nothing to fear.

My clothes were torn and shredded into useless rags on the floor. A new group of more intent hands held themselves above my head. A violent snap brought my eyes upward only to be blurred by a milky thick stream falling from fresh wounds in the bark coated skin of the pallid branches. Leaves acting as brushes painted the fluid over my body, cleansing away every imperfection until they lowered me shimmering to the ground.

A rush of vertigo shook my balance, while the fireplace withdrew into the wall without shrinking in the distance. The room stretched away and raced toward me at the same time. Miss Ann lay on her back, out of focus behind a blur of wind dancing ashes. She breathed in deeply and exhaled thousands more of the small charcoal colored fragments — now only smears wiped from all definition, her hand reached for me. I took one step forward feeling the crackle of dry leaves underfoot.

"You are welcomed here Ro." Miss Ann winked at me revealing dark eyes the color of dead wood. "Come down into the Sunday hole boy."

Around us, the room faded into transparency. Trees swayed gently side to side, dropping their finger leaves. Shallow pits in the shape of leaves randomly sunk their depressions around her body. From the wounds, she leaked the same gelatinous milk now oozing over my skin. My nose flared around the sweet smell of wine and berries.

"Bring him this Ro." Without any visible signs of motion she yanked to a seated position, dirt and leaves falling from the skin on her back. I reached out feeling the rough bark dig into my skin. "When we are complete, you must. Promise me."

Standing, her toes dug downward, rooting her into the ashy foundations. "I need you to trust me. Can you do that?"

Her fingers shot forward into my chest, through bark-skin and bone. Tendrils embraced my heart, wrapping tightly around the vital organ. The lifelong rhythm song of its beat muted. My own body became silent to me for the first time. Now hushed, I realized how loudly the song reverberated throughout my entire life. A soundtrack playing in the background of every moment, day and night. Asleep and awake, the cadence of my body marched me forward.

No longer masked by the volume of blood hissing here to there, my senses opened. I heard chattering squirrels on a rooftop three houses away and understood their complaints about the stale dog food dropped in the yard below. A colony of ants stripping bites from a dead rat argued if their queen really appreciated the hard work it took bringing her food every day of their short lives.

"You can hear the soft melody of blue now. Listen to red's sharp call." Disbelief screamed from gut instincts. Colors don't make sounds. But she was right. I heard the melody of hue and harmonies of shades. I could feel sounds of the sky and taste the sweet tang of happiness. The bitter sting of anger pierced my tongue then soothed by love's creamy freshness. New senses grew in and around me.

"Bring him the hands." She pointed to the carriage across the room full to the rim with charred plastic limbs. "To feel the shape."

I gently placed strips of bark in the carriage on top of the plastic hands. Then the alarm clock buzzed me awake.

8

CALLER I.D.

I GUESS WHEN MOM STARTED HER MORNING the next day the world looked exactly the same as any other day. I mean why would anything be different? She probably rolled out of bed while Dad was still shooting chainsaw snores at the ceiling. Her pink yoga mat was still unfolded in the middle of the living room floor when I left for school so she must've used it, right?

"See you tonight, Dad." The pastel light glowing around his studio door was my only answer, echoing through the yard as I ran to make it to class before the bell. Most days he wore his cartoonishly enormous nineteen seventies headphones when he worked in the morning. He hated listening to music with ear buds stuffed in. He told me once they made it sound like tin cans and strings.

The empty carriage lay on its side in the middle of a pile of drying leaves under the window. I must have brought it home from Miss Ann's, but the memory hid wrapped in a deep black somewhere in the back of my mind. Whatever he was making, the charred plastic baby arms seemed a bit on the dark side for a public piece to me, but I wasn't the artist or the patron. If the school was expecting something happy fun joy, they had another thing coming. In the few days I'd known Miss Ann, my bet is she had something in mind to ruffle up tight feathers rather than pacify conservative family value types anyway.

I didn't know Dad wouldn't answer the phone while I was at school. I wouldn't find out until later that the tippy toers would be left stranded in the parking lot outside Mom's locked studio. Apparently dozens of messages were left on her unchecked voicemail wondering "Did you cancel class today?" "I don't remember anything about a schedule change." "Where are you?" Her clockwork organizational regimen never deviated allowing the rest of Pastor's families to plan their lives with relative ease around where their little girls could be found on any given day.

When she didn't answer her phone, calls fell to our house machine. Dad kept an extension line in his studio, but he rarely picked up unless it was a number he recognized. Since it wasn't mom's cell or my school calling, he either didn't think they were worth interrupting his work, or the ringer wasn't switched on. I never did ask which.

Before I was taken back to Miss Ann's house again, I wanted to tell my parents about the trees again. To convince them I wasn't crazy. I heard the muffled sound of T-Rex's fuzzed out guitars pumping through the closed windows of dad's studio. Locked. I pounded against the metal door, bruising my knuckles and drawing blood from cracking skin.

A shadow slid across the door. I jumped to my right to escape the branch's crackly grip. Sprinting across the grass, I headed for the house. My only chance was to get inside a closet or next to an inner wall away from the windows and doors.

With no time to react, a root bulged upward from the ground catching my foot mid-flight. I tumbled face first expecting to smash my nose into the brick patch between the grass and the side of the house. Instead, my momentum halted and I was hoisted into the air by a long, leaf-covered appendage.

The sound of "20th Century Boy" spinning on Dad's record player followed me up the block before the trees turned left on Independence Lane.

9

FLY AWAY HOME

I PASSED THE CARRIAGE ALREADY EMPTIED and parked on Miss Ann's porch and knocked on the screen door. Letting myself in, I slipped my shoes off before walking in. Long and sheer, the curtains danced in front of the tall, open windows. My skin shivered into bumps feeling a cold breeze in the house I failed to notice outside. The floor held its creaks and groans quiet beneath my feet. The reserved, hesitant pause in the house seemed out of place compared to the vibrancy and restless energy of my last few visits.

"Miss Ann?" Muffled, no echo bounced between the walls and up the stairs. I wrapped my fingers around the ornately carved owl head at the bottom of the banister. A sharp pain pierced the long strip of skin between my thumb and index finger. I jerked my arm away inserting the wound directly into my mouth. Bitter and metallic, the taste of blood flooded over my tongue. A long shanked splinter pushed the skin up from the lowest wrinkle of my thumb all the way to the line of life.

I grabbed the end of the splinter with my teeth, chewing it free while the owl head shook dust from its finely carved feathers and shut its beak before returning to the lifeless pose near the bottom of the staircase. I chuckled at the impossibility that I was sure climbed from the playful imagination in the back of my mind.

"Hello?" I rubbed blood on my jeans and threw the splinter at the owl head out of spite. Straining my eyes to see into the shadows, I flipped the nearest light switch up. A bright pop shot through the air, and a spark lit up behind the switch. The bulbs remained dark and powerless. Swimming and casting odd shapes over the walls and floor, the only illumination came from between the windows billowing curtains.

"Hello?" I called out again to no one and turned around in circles, not wanting to go further into the house without Miss Ann. Half way around in my second spin, I stopped. She changed the pictures. They were hung in the same places, with the same frames void of any personality. The black and white images still showed the old tree in all its cracked detail with the furniture scattered around the yard and the cringe inspiring stuffed animal hanging in the tire swing. The frames butted up against the ceiling, cutting off the image in the same strange point as the other pictures only now, the headless people were all gone.

My head jerked around at a squeak from the kitchen and my chest all but exploded.

"Hello Ro." Miss Ann sat in a wheelchair, looking up at me smiling wildly from the entrance to the living room. "I'm sorry. Have you been here long?"

"No. Not long." I absently rubbed at the wounded skin on my hand. "Are you alright? What happened?" Her torso curled forward slightly, held up by long, unpadded wooden armrests. Unlike the wheelchairs I was used to seeing, this particular chair was made entirely of wood, from the short handles on the back of the seat to the wheels themselves. Carvings of distorted faces and barren landscapes covered every visible area of its surface.

"No no. I'm fine as wine kiddo." Miss Ann tilted her head and winked. The bun on the side of her head, so tightly done in our previous meetings shifted slightly lower near to her ear. "Sometimes these old legs need a break is all." She gave a light tug to the edge of the powder blue comforter over her thighs. I caught a glimpse showing what looked like dry bark instead of skin before she folded her hands in her lap.

"If you're sure." My knees trembled as the fireplace came into view around the corner.

"Everything okay Ro?" Miss Ann reached out for my hand. I yanked away at the feel of rough skin. "Don't go disappearing on me now kiddo."

I looked into her eyes, so generous and kind. Hesitant to make me even more nervous, she brushed a finger over the dark purple knitted scarf around her neck. "Remember Ro, you are welcome here."

"Why?" I backed out of the room so I wouldn't have to keep looking at the fireplace.

"We are connected you and me." Without touching the wheels, the chair turned to face me. "I promise there is nothing here that will ever hurt you."

"You said that before."

"I know." She opened her arms drawing me into an embrace. "I know."

Fighting against the urge to turn tail and disappear, I fell to my knees and buried my head on her lap. The soft comforter covered my face; the smell of oranges, cedar and freshly cut grass drowned my senses. My lips parted slightly allowing stiff twigs to slip into my mouth and down my throat. I pushed back against the taste of dirt, but the gag reflex was too weak to repel the hungry invaders. Her arms squeezed harder than an old woman of any dream or possible imagining. Breath squeezed from my lungs as I struggled to free myself. I couldn't open my eyes against the pressure of her legs. No way to scream. No way to escape.

Thick mud clogged my tear ducts making it impossible for tears to drop. Even if they had, the moisture would have been absorbed by the thick cotton of the blanket before it ran down my cheeks. A soft humming swelled from her belly.

I'd never heard the song, but the melody rose and fell in a familiar rollercoaster.

"Ladybug ladybug," she beckoned the words from my head, stealing their meaning. "Fly away home."

Her arms opened wide and I teetered on to my side in front of her bare feet. The footrest's wooden supports creaked at the shift in her weight. From below, the angles of her face took on an air of royalty. Through grinning teeth, she drew in a breath pulling me forward against her shins.

"Come with me Ro." The voice, full and deep, seemed to come from behind, pushing me forward into the living room. "As you can see, I need you to be my legs today. Ready for some walkin'?"

Miss Ann's hands folded softly atop her lap, the wheelchair rolled forward creaking and snapping under its own strange will. Turning in front of the fireplace, it stopped, leaving Miss Ann facing in my direction. The bun wound tightly on the side of her head, wiggled at the wheel's sudden stop.

My hands shook. I pushed myself to my feet, knees threatening to buckle me down to the floor again. When she winked, a wave of harmless calm rippled across the floor spreading over me. A low lit flame warmed in the hearth behind her chair outlining Miss Ann in a glimmering orange. Watching in awe, I would have done anything for her at that moment.

"Ro, we must do terrible things now." The smile vanished from her face. My heart shattered seeing the awful sadness creep into her. "But if we squeeze our lemons, we can find sweet through the bitter.

"Nann's already weaving her laces. Your daddy needs a leg." Jumping from her wheelchair, a schoolgirl's energy sprung in her step. "Are you ready kiddo?"

I nodded. I didn't want to be, but I was ready.

A void opened in the fire again. Through the rising heat vapors, the beautiful tree shimmered out of focus in a miasma of shifting, glowing color. She floated through the hole rather than walking. Her legs melted to streaks of purple and deep blue watercolor.

"Miss Ann?" I hesitated at the blistering threshold of the fireplace.

Come through Ro. Come through. I'd never heard the voice before. Not with my ears. So familiar though. As close to me as if I were talking to myself. *Squeeze your lemons Ro.*

Squeeze.

My feet walked over the smoking embers and I was gone.

10

GIRL FIGHTING I
April 1973

THE MAN SAT ON THE FLOOR, leaning against a wall stunned and terrified. Blood drooling down from both corners of his mouth sputtered and splashed as he worked his lips up and down in silence. The cuts in his chest pierced between the ribs and deep into his lungs. Already half filled with syrupy red liquid, he would soon drown completely in his own fluids.

"Why?" His whisper gurgled and popped as the air forced its way up through his broken throat. His eyes searched for a reason in the young girl's sweet face.

"It has to be this way. Daddy said so." She leaned down wiping the blade clean on his shoulder. Snow gloves prevented any fingerprints from marking the brown striped, sweat-darkened leather handle.

She turned her head as the faintest whine of sirens arrived through the storming wind outside. "I have to go now."

He moved his hand leaving a smear in the bloody puddle pooling next to him. Backing away before he could touch her, the girl shivered in the cold. Then she stood still, rooted to her spot until the quiet whistling of his struggling breath ended. The knife fell from her hand, clattering between his dead legs, blade pointing away from his groin.

She opened the sliding glass door at the back of the house. Carried on the wind, the police sirens howled louder, closer. She lowered her chin to her chest and closed her eyes. Her voice trembled with signs of guilt and sadness. "One for one that is how it must be. One leaf falls one takes root on the tree."

11

VERNON & CORY
March 1973

THE PRISONER SAT UPRIGHT ON THE CELL FLOOR, legs extended straight ahead, knees flat. Lieutenant Vernon Heathrow rocked on his heels outside of the bars impatiently waiting for an answer.

"I asked you a question Branch." Vernon hid the anxiety in his voice beneath years of training and experience dealing with psychos like Cory Branch.

No part of Cory's body moved other than the corners of his mouth as he grinned. As quickly as the facial expression arrived, it returned to the blankness stretching down from his closed eyes.

"I know you're not stupid enough to believe I'm going to hurt you myself. But, I can pull some strings to put you in gen pop. They'd just love to get their hands on a fuckwad like you. Those guys just love playing with monsters like you who have a thing for hurting kids." Vernon tapped his finger on the nearest iron pole, hoping to elicit some form of reaction from the prisoner.

"Vernon, I've already given you the answer to your question." Cory's voice was high-pitched and full of gravel. Exactly the sound you would expect from the worm thin, moist and pale little man. "It might not be what you wanted to hear, but it's the only one I've got."

"Cory, the only place those stupid rhymes make any sense is in that perverted, drug addled brain of yours." Vernon squeezed the bars and kicked with his steel-toed boot. The ring echoed in a sharp wave across the shining, polished floor. "I need you to tell me why you killed those people."

"One for one that is how it must be. One leaf falls one takes root on the tree."

"One for one." Vernon slipped his thumbs underneath the dark red suspenders his girlfriend Michelle made him wear. She had a thing against belts. The trail of rectangular scars on her back explained to him wordlessly why she hated them so. "Let's do some math together then. Shall we? I count seven people you killed, that we know of so far. I'm betting the deeper I poke around, the more I find." Cory stared into space, unmoved by the threatening tone of the burly and angry detective.

"Let me just go pick out ten of our friends from the yard who's uncle sneaked into their rooms and touched them the wrong way late at night. I bet they could find a few exciting ways to pass the time with you. Or should I bring twelve? Thirteen?" Vernon called back over his shoulder, hand on the door.

"My family."

"What did you say?"

"...to protect my family...one for one..."

"From who?"

"...to keep them safe...one leaf falls..."

"Safe from who Branch?"

"...no other way...one takes root..."

"On the tree. So you said."

"...on the tree..."

"Tell me who you need to protect your family from? I can help."

"You don't want to do that Vernon."

"Yes." Vernon squatted next to the bars, his knees creaking from years of catcher's cartilage. "I do Cory."

"I wouldn't do that." Cory twisted wiry legs beneath himself and crawled next to the bars of the cell.

"If someone made you do these things...if they threatened your family...I can help you. Tell me."

"I wouldn't do that to you. Not to my worst enemy." His head smashed into the bars so quickly, the Lieutenant had no chance to react.

"Open twelve!" Vernon screamed. "Branch, stop! Open twelve goddammit!" The door at the end of the hall flew open. Boots stomped on the hard polished floor in rapid succession, running. Cory's forehead caved in by the third blow. A smattering of blood sprayed across Vernon's white shirt. "Stop Branch... I can help you." No one was left to hear him.

Vernon watched Cory Branch fall backward until his head touched the floor. The key to the cell moved in slow motion slipping home into the locking mechanism. When questioned later by his supervising officers, Vernon didn't mention how Cory's body righted itself, smiled with a broken, leaking mouth and smashed into the bars for one final wet smack. This sloppy soundtrack to the lifeless expression in his eyes and marionette looseness of his limbs flickered through the home movie projections Vernon witnessed every time his eyes closed. He knew Cory Branch was already dead before sitting up that last time. There was no way to prove it, but he knew.

1 2

CE N'EST PAS LE MONDE

or

THE BIG MIDNIGHT

SHE WALKED THREE FEET IN FRONT OF ME. My fingertips brushed against the ends of her long, dark blond hair rolling between the brightly colored leaves that floated between us. Short bolts of electricity sparked, charging through my hand. Not unpleasant, the sneeze-like release of tension coursed over my body urging me forward.

I tried to close the gap, she matched every long stride and jump keeping her distance. The wind laughed with Miss Ann's voice. Her head turned revealing through whipping strands of atypically unkempt hair, a comely grin and winking eye. The familiar wrinkled face retreated against the years. White hair recaptured youthful glow. Skin tightened over sprightly muscles and liver spots vanished. I knew this young woman flirting me onward. I knew this beautiful girl. Everything in her physical appearance retreated backward into who she once was long before we'd met.

This woman was now a teenager with a freshly unexplored body. This girl was yet uneaten by the hungry world's never satiated desire to devour all vibrant sparkle from her eyes. Her eyes. Miss Anne didn't hide deep within the gorgeous rolling ocean of blues. Nothing could disguise the passion for life that glowed in her eyes. Adrianna Heathrow was home. My home. I wondered what I looked like to her.

She turned and faced me. I stopped running. Hands on hips, she kicked at the tall grass growing so swiftly around her bare feet.

Picking a dandelion, she looked up at my face. I dissolved into a pool of warm goo in her rapturous gaze.

"I wondered when you'd stop." She blew on the flower sending a white cloud of seeds scattering between the long uncut green blades. "Oops. I forgot to make a wish."

"Wishes don't come true anyway." Regret often appears before the words finish leaving our mouths.

"Really?" She gently leaned back into the soft grass leaving no sign of her save the indentation of her body outline. Her voice came up from the negative space between the reaching blades, "That's really sad. The way you see life Ro? My wishes come true all the time."

"Sure they do." I wanted to believe her. Life already provided me with many bricks and mortar to build up my walls against that hope.

"You're here with me now." Her head reappeared. She winked again and threw a handful of grass at me, watching with raised eyebrows as the torn, flimsy green strands blew away in the wind. "Go ahead Ro. Close your eyes and make a wish."

"What? No."

"I'll bet it comes true." A light blue spark of electricity shot from her fingers into mine, molecules between us before she grabbed my hand. "I'll bet you a kiss."

"Right."

"With tongue?" She leaned her head to the side and winked again.

"Don't do that."

"Don't do what?"

"That." I pointed a limp finger and mimicked a melodramatic reflection of her flirt.

"Why not?" She did it again. "Don't you like it?"

"Yeah." I looked down at my toes digging into the soft dirt. "That's the problem." My cheek burned at the touch of her fingers. With every intention of pulling away, I closed my eyes and surrendered instead.

"Go ahead Ro." Her body pressed against mine. "I dare you. Make a wish."

Before I could rearrange my thoughts into anything resembling coherency, her hand pulled the back of my head down. Our mouths melted us into one person. I imagined my left leg kicking up in the air behind me driven by the magnitude of her eroticism. Oxygen flushed through my pours. My entire body opened itself feeling solid and *real*. Images of the two of us sharing life flickered through my mind in a slide show of overexposed black and white hopeful possibilities.

I don't remember the name of the girl who gave me my first kiss. I do know it was New Year's Eve. I didn't have a thing for her, and I don't think she liked me either. We were decent friends and for lack of being invited to any other parties that year, I went to her house to help babysit her little sister. An unspoken tension drowned us in the living room while we watched Dick Clark breathing steam clouds in Times Square. Conversation was nonexistent. I'd look at her on the other end of the sofa and turn away soon as she looked back. She played the same "I'm not looking at you" game with me.

We both knew The Big Midnight was coming soon. Shy with no experience in this sort of thing at all, I waited for her to take the reins and get it over with. At 11:52, I picked up her limp limbed sleeping little sister and put her to bed. The girl was waiting for me back in the unlit hallway. Her weight shifting heel to toe. Not pretty, but not ugly, the television glow lit her from behind and I found myself attracted to her in a way I didn't think I ever would have been.

She clumsily shoved her arms around my neck and planted one on me. Hard. Teeth slammed painfully into my gums, her tongue stabbed between my lips darting stiffly side to side searching for a drop of water in the Sahara. Despite my better judgment, I got hard. My heart sprinted, hands exploring her underdeveloped chest and pulling the thin dress over her underwear. I squeezed. Flat and bony, her ass didn't match up with the soft curves I fantasized about while reading the dirty magazines a pack of us guys hid beneath that one special bush on the path to school.

This memory existed in an entirely different universe. Adrianna made me whole. It never occurred to me that who I thought I'd been up until this point in my life would be inconsequential compared to the Me I would be when she touched me. I knew why the poets dreamed of angels. I knew why Paris sacrificed his world for Helena. Romeo and Juliet weren't some selfish, stubborn teenagers in a play anymore. For the first time in my life, I lived.

Lungs burning, the instinct to breathe battled and defeated my desire. I pulled away. I understood what it meant to die at the splitting of our lips. One thin strand of saliva stretched between our mouths shimmering in the bright light of the world. She wiped it away with the back of her hand and I wanted to cry. Her head tipped to the side again and I winked before she could. We both laughed.

A flush climbed up my head doubling my vision and muffling my ears. She grabbed my shoulders and steadied my feet. A hint of concern spread over her face, but left quicker than it came.

"Sorry." She looked down.

"For what?" She could've shot me through the spleen with a rusted arrow and not needed to apologize at that moment.

"I've been wanting to do that since we got here." Her cheeks turned bright pink. "Maybe you think it's weird."

"Not at all." I squeezed her hands. "Besides, you granted a wish I didn't know I had."

"Yeah?"

"Yeah."

"Well alright." She turned, running off through the field. "Come on then."

"Where are we?" We ran for what seemed like hours. I should have been winded. "What is this place?"

She didn't turn, a laughing voice drifted behind the bounce of her hair. "We're down the Sunday hole kiddo."

"What?" I stopped running after her. Two trees stood tall at the top of a rolling hill to my left. Adrianna grew smaller in their shadow becoming part of their shape. Their multicolored leaves absorbed the bounce of her hair and took up the dance after she vanished from sight.

I took a step in their direction and fell through the world. My stomach lurched, spinning and twisting into knots. The trees remained in place, grass swayed around me. The sun hung high in the pure blue sky and the horizon line held court in every direction.

I fell until I reached the edge of the shadows by the trees. From the deep, negative darkness, she glided forward and hugged me. "You are welcome here," then kissed my cheek.

When I exploded, there was no pain. I was nowhere and everywhere. I felt nothing and everything. With no eyes, I saw in between and through. Having no ears I listened to the unwritten melodies of the universe. With no arms, I held her inside of myself no longer needing boundaries between separate bodies.

"Welcome Ro." The voiceless trees sang.

"You are welcome in this place." I fell from branches along seeds and leaves.

"You are welcome in me." There were no lips to kiss or arms to embrace.

"This is not the world."

Landing face first on the hard floor, I woke in my bedroom. Stars remained high in the sky through a hole in the curtains. Hyperventilating, my head swam in circles unable to focus my eyes on anything. I sat back against my bed, naked feet coated in dark black mud.

Sweating, my cold skin hurt all over. I dragged the bottoms of my feet along the carpet leaving smears of dirt. I lifted myself to a sitting position on the edge of the bed and slid my hands under the covers behind me. She breathed in deep and rolled over. The girl's face glowed through the dark. I knew every inch of skin and strand of hair. I felt the sheet slide over her dirt covered toes. Before, I thought I understood what beautiful meant. This is how beautiful felt.

Remarkably, I wasn't surprised. We were together.

13

STAPLEFACE
Girlfighting II

CRUMPLED INTO A FETAL BALL ON THE GROUND, the first thought that came to his mind wasn't how do I defend myself from the next blow? Or, even the one after that? Arthur Hill was actually happy — happy that nobody was around to watch him get shellacked by a kid.

"You hit like a girl." The tooth he spit out landed in a small splotch of blood on the drab green, office carpet. Arthur tried to laugh, but it hurt. It really fucking hurt.

"Mm hm." Her fingers intertwined with his long greasy hair yanking his head back. She cocked her right arm above her thin shoulder and held it in place, making sure he opened his eyes. She wanted him to see the blow coming. When it did, the viper lashed out quick and fierce. Cartilage was pulverized and bone cracked, flattening the remains of his nose level with his bloodshot cheeks.

He fell backward, knees bent beneath him. Laughing through the spurts of blood spouting from his mouth, he rolled on his side and coughed. She pulled her right foot back to kick him in the stomach, but he saw it coming. He swiped at her left leg bringing her down to the floor with an air-stealing thump, hitting her shoulder on the mahogany desk.

Before she could catch her breath he was on top of her, pinning her arms down under his shins. He followed the dripping blood with two quick punches to the forehead, he didn't care that he was fighting a girl. If he didn't put a stop to this soon, she could kill him. He saw the inhumane look of her dark blue pupil-less eyes. No reason or compassion. Venom.

She struggled beneath the weight of him. He had more than a hundred pounds on her, plus the years he spent studying martial arts. Her surprise attack was the only way she gained the upper hand. Why would he ever expect anything like this from a girl? Now that he had stolen that element, she would need to play this out much smarter if she wanted to beat him.

Why me?

Arthur didn't enjoy fighting. The target of every bully and thug since grade school, he accepted it as part of daily life. By the time he turned eight he was sneaking out of the house to sneak into the beginners Ju-Jitsu class at the Y down the street. Miming the teacher's moves in his bedroom and watching every training video he could find, he slowly learned how to feel his body as a weapon.

The first time Arthur fought back was a disaster. Marcus Johansen stood a head and a half taller, and had thirty pounds on him. It didn't help that his three cronies were more than willing to get their licks in too. But the most important weapon Arthur learned was patience. As the bruises healed, he studied. He practiced. He punched the old tree in his backyard until his knuckles fell numb and calluses grew over the scabs. He didn't hide or wait for them to come after him again.

He forged his father's signature on the note from school. Dad was too drunk to pay attention to Arthur anyway. Marcus' broken jaw and ripped ear prevented any further bullying for the rest of elementary school. They knew better than to fuck with him now.

He threw himself forward with an elbow to the girl's throat. Connected properly, she would be out and it would all be over. He could relax and call the police. She was smart though. She read his move and twisted to the side. His elbow grazed off the side of her cheek and crashed into the floor.

Arthur howled. The trapped animal in him cried out in terror. Her teeth ripped deep into his bicep. A chunk of his muscle and tissue hung from between her lips. He went limp to the floor holding his now painfully useless limb. She shoved him away and stood over him. She spit, the meat splattered on the ground next to his head. He squeezed his eyes tight to fight off the pain. Seeing nothing but a bright warning yellow, he realized the girl was not finished with him yet.

He heard the sound of metal clanking together. Sharp pressure from bony knees came down on his chest. His eyes opened to the last image they would ever see. The stapler made sure of that.

14

NEW MORNING EYES

"YOU'RE LEAVING?" Her new morning eyes opened and followed my stumble into the desk, jockeying with my pants. "I didn't peg you as the wham bam thank you ma'am type.""

"I need to find Ace." I picked the shirt on top of the laundry pile, paying no attention to the abstract spatter of tomato sauce painted like blood down the center. "He's never been gone this long before."

"Like I said," Miss Ann fingered a swirl of hair behind her ear. "A dog like him will never find a better place to run around and dig for goodies than in the Sunday." She stretched a sleepy hand for me. The blanket shifted further down her arm revealing the wonderful perfect curve of a breast. My resistance fled behind the surge of hormonal want.

"Miss Ann." The comforter rolled from her shoulders. Not shying away, she bared her body, a feast for my eyes. Her skin chiseled the thoughts in my head, carving them away from their original intent. I hung on tightly for fear of losing myself in the beautiful distraction. "How did you get here?"

"Does it matter?" Her shoulders shrugged. "The Unfading wants us to be together. I can only guess why." She stood on the mattress digging her toes into the rumpled sheets. I looked up seeing what appeared to be thin vines swirling inside her perfectly shaped nostrils. I cringed at the thought before the hair moving with her breath came into focus. "They know enough to understand you wouldn't be interested in shacking it up with the ancient old lady. So they returned a younger me." With a subtle flourish, her hands traced the outline of her figure.

Years looking at pictures online and daydreaming about what a naked girl would feel like didn't substitute in the slightest for the real thing. I inhaled a trembling breath, struggling to calm my nerves. Miss

Ann slipped from the bed. Her naked, smooth and supple body stood inches from me.

"You're going to love me Ro." She laughed. "That's not such a bad thing is it?" I shook my head.

"I guess not." She took my hands and placed them on her waist. Her softness gave a little at my touch. My palms relished in the warmth of another person's temperature. Fingers explored downward over the waves of her hips. I lingered at the small diagonal crux between thigh and waist before letting my arms fall limp.

"Then why are you shaking like a doodlebug?" She wrapped her arms around my neck and pulled me close. Every molecule was fully aware of her body pressing against me with nothing between us but a stained t-shirt. Nuzzling her mouth into my neck, the warm breath sent a calm ripple down my body erasing the shivers in its wake. "I'm here Ro. I'm here for you."

Time is an imperfect system of division, sliced into precise seconds, minutes, hours, years... No matter how infinitely we attempt to measure its passing, no matter how intricately wound the tool we use, clocks are not exact. Some moments flash by so quickly they can scarcely be traced. Other moments exist for an eternity. The excruciating lifetime of the second hand's crawl as it nears the twelve on the last day of school. Three months of summer vacation for an eleven year old snap away in but a moment. Though her kiss will remain on my lips until I acknowledge I might not have existed at all before her, the fast-forward of that morning refuses to slow even in my memory.

15

FAKE FAKE PLASTIC TREES

YOU KNOW WHEN YOU FALL ASLEEP with your head on your hands and wake up to the prickling of a million tiny pins and needles? That's how my hands felt. I walked through a hole in the world and came out the other side wearing invisible gloves filled with moist sand. Fingers thick as poorly wrapped sausages drenched in warm water.

The maple trees hanging over the window creaked in the wind. Leaves suckled at the warm teat of a loving and generous sun. The too blindingly bright red feathers of a cardinal stood firm on a branch singing territorial warnings.

A painful numbness expanded along my arms and legs coming to unrest in fingers and toes. I reached for her side of the bed and found nothing there. Cold, empty sheets and an indented pillow replaced Miss Ann's warm body. I stumbled from the bed unable to stand. The clenching muscles in my gut folding my body into a twisted, agonizing origami.

Jaw popping with strain, I forced my torso open and pulled a pair of sweatpants over my legs. This was difficult to do since my feet refused to leave the floor. Only able to breathe in short, staccato spurts, I hooked my t-shirt with a crooked finger and dragged the stained pre-shrunken tail along behind.

I twisted the front door knob and pulled it open letting light from the outside world into the house. Behind me, the deafening roar of swirling water swirling down a drain sucked at the surrounding air. Compelled forward by the image of Ace's face in my rattling mind and the scent of a freshly mowed lawn from the neighbor's yard, my torso muscles slowly released. Blood once again flowing, my legs took the hint, advancing recklessly faster with every step. I opened my mouth to call out for the dog.

"Ro?" Rather than the accustomed timbres of my own vibrating chords, Miss Anne's voice bounced in echoes from closed garage doors and rolled up car windows. "Where are you?" She leaned from the doorway magnificently naked, searching down the street in the opposite direction from me. In my peripheral I saw what used to be the old maple in our front yard, lean down, thick branches lifting her from the house. The clear sheen and rough edges of the poorly made, injection molded giant plastic tree folded and creaked.

A spark of sunlight reflected from the leaves — too bright to be from the softness of natural materials. Clicking and scratching pricked at my ears from the hard surfaces of the imitation plants rubbing together. Lines etched down from the corners of Miss Anne's mouth tracing below her jaw. Her plasticized chin slid straight down against her breastbone, the mouth nothing but a black hole rectangle. The branch disappeared into the middle of her back, operating Miss Ann's movements and melodramatic facial expressions. Robotically stiff. A nightmarish ventriloquism.

Landing on the sidewalk in front of me, a leaf clattered and bounced. Stiff and unbending, the shimmer of reflected light from the plastic blinded me for a moment. My legs continued running despite losing my sense of direction for a moment. It became more difficult to move my feet through the weight piling up on top of them. The scraping and cracking made my spine scream with each step forward.

When the glare spots dimmed, a mountain of plastic leaves in my path grew into focus. Browns and yellows and reds and greens blanketed to the end of the street ahead. Vein maps and stems raised in stiff lines from jagged, imperfectly cut surfaces. Flat excess strips, missed by the press blade hung imperfectly over random edges. Some of the leaves were stamped with the words "Made In The USA" in bold recessed letters. Ahead of me, leaves dropped from branches adding to the height and thickness of the pile. Every step was more exerting than the last. Sweating despite the coolness of the morning, I pushed forward.

Swelling larger by the second, the mountain of fake leaves matched the height of my waist before I reached the end of the next driveway. A white minivan sped past on the street unimpeded by the tree's shedding. In its wake, waves of more leaves crashed down burying me to the shoulders — heavy and grabbing me from every angle, I could not move. I was cocooned in a maple scented burial mound.

"Don't go now Ro. Your little puppy is sweet and fine in the Sunday. Cross my heart and spit on a..." Her voice was warbled and tinny. The branch stuck in the middle of her back shook with each syllable. "...compass rose."

The tree covered in knots and dripping white sap, lowered Miss Ann close enough that I could smell the syrup sticking to her legs. No longer young, the old woman turned ventriloquist puppet was covered in deeply carved shadowy wrinkles. Eyebrows pressed into the molded flesh of her shiny forehead and crawled high above the unfocused dead eyes. She looked surprised at my escape attempt.

"You're going to love me Ro. Don't you want to love me?" I twisted my head away, my chin pushing a trough in the leaves. Her dry lips landed against the corner of my mouth and onto the cheek. Her snakelike tongue slithered across my skin leaving a trail of burning spittle, leaving a bubbling swath in its wake. "Loving me is good. Come on... love."

Bacon-scented smoke curled in random shapes around my face. The sickly spiced tang entwined with the agony of melting skin. My unsteady mind wobbled, toppling over the cliff's edge into confusion. Hundreds more leaves clattered on top of me inflating the funeral pile. My screams drowned to silence by the shuffling, grating synthetic plants. Despite the pain and revulsion, I salivated at the scent of cooking meat.

One fake leaf slipped against the burning strip on my face imbedding itself into place. Seeping into the skin, the too-bright green glistened along with my wet, melting skin. Bubbles grew from the top epidermal layer, tiny rainbows of refracted light striping around their curves. They popped shooting droplets of misty pink over the surrounding artificial foliage.

My mouth opened wide to howl in dread and pain. Blocking the outward burst of air, hundreds of wire thin vines crawled into the opening and down my throat. I gagged, as every morsel of food fighting to climb up my throat was shoved back down by the thrashing creepers. Coils lined my innards. Unceasing, they continued to drive into me. My skin tore beyond its fragile limitations. Rips shredded open. Stiff, leafy claws sharpened to diamond edges grasped inside the holes. Pieces of me floated to the top of the sickly swelling mountain. Carried away on the surface, leaving behind trails of pale, transparent syrup on the leaves.

My eyes opened. Miss Ann lay next to me resting her cheek on her hand watching me.

"How were your sleeps?"

"Down the Sunday Hole"
will continue…

AUTHOR'S NOTE

Earlier versions of
"The loneliness of Left Field"
originally appeared in
Unusual Stories Vol. 1

and

"Josephine"
appeared in
Black Lantern Publishing No. 8

ACKNOWLEDGMENTS

Katrina M. Randall
(Through some miracle of genius, you make it seem like I know
what I'm doing with this whole writing thing),

Emily Duncan, Jesse James Freeman, Cathy Shaw, Greg Simanson &
Katherine Fye Sears for opening the possibilities.

The North Scituate Library, Steven R. Porter and ARIA, DS George-
Jones, Gordon Bonnet, Stephanie K. Fuller

Mom

Jodi
(Thanks for not killing me in the back seat on those long car rides.)

Melissa, Jonah & Gabriel
Life with you is the greatest story in the world
I love you forever and ever
NO MATTER WHAT

MORE GREAT READS
FROM BOOKTROPE

The Key to Everything by **Alex Kimmell** (Thriller) When Auden discovers a curious leather-bound book, its contents will soon endanger his entire family. The pages of this book draw him into a prison that cannot be breached, a place that can only be unlocked with a very special key.

Phobia by **Daniel Lance Wright** (Thriller) Heights, crowds, small spaces... How does a psychologist handle three phobia sufferers on a cruise ship in the Gulf of Mexico when the ship is overtaken by Lebanese terrorists?

Pacific Sun and Other Stories by **Cris Markos** (Short Stories) Pacific Sun and Other Stories explores the extremes of the human experience: from genocide and human trafficking to poverty and terminal illness. From Bosnia to Kentucky, these stories inflect the best and worst of the human psyche.

The Art of Work by **Phaye Poliakoff-Chen** (Short Stories) Darkly funny stories about chronic do-gooders who battle their way toward understanding, careening between resentment and fulfillment.

Four Rubbings by **Jennifer L. Hotes** (Young Adult Thriller) Fourteen-year old Jose, haunted by the death of her mother, leads her best friends to an ancient cemetary to rub graves on Halloween night. Convinced she will come away with proof of her mother's spirit at last,her journey and that of her friends takes a very different turn.

Discover more books and learn about our
new approach to publishing at **booktrope.com**.

CPSIA information can be obtained at www.ICGtesting.com
Printed in the USA
LVOW08s0745110614

389561LV00001B/73/P

9 781620 151839